Advance

Benton masterfully weaves together the travails and tragedy of an African family, enmeshed in Zimbabwean politics, with the daily routines of a Southern California child development center confronting a murder and kidnapping. It works as a mystery. The uniqueness is in the portrayal of the director of the child care center as a caring professional and a master sleuth. A compelling story. *Belle Cole and David Wilson*

Set in a California Child Development Center, this story of a young African family's struggle in a strange new culture will absorb early childhood educators and mystery lovers alike. *Marion Cushman, former child development center director*

From the discovery of a dead bunny to a fatal bicycle "accident" involving a Zimbabwean family in the child care center, Hannah, the center's director, acts and reflects and responds caringly to her staff and parents, musing all the while on the challenges of providing quality care to young children in a diverse and changing, and sometimes dangerous, world. *Elizabeth Jones, Faculty, Human Development, Pacific Oaks College, Pasadena, California*

A mystery for ECE professionals who care deeply about young children and enjoy fiction with a twist of international intrigue. *Crucial Time*, set primarily in a preschool-child care center, is a tale with many layers. *Nancy Richard, author of* A Small Steadying Sail of Love

In this story of kidnapping and betrayal, as well as love, early childhood educators will recognize the complexity of forces within their day care centers, which they must face on a daily basis. *Pauline Crabb, former teacher and college administrator*

Ms. Benton knows the worlds of child day care and academia well and has woven an engrossing tale from the many strands. We were thoroughly entertained and educated about Early Childhood Education in one fell swoop. It can't get better than that! *Janet and Casey Howell*

An original work that reminds us just how much can change in an instant. Into a new and confusing setting of a different country, comes a young family from Zimbabwe. Set in a children's pre-school around the disappearance of a small boy, politics and personalities play out in inventive details. *Carolyn Carpenter, former teacher*

Early Childhood Education in Pasadena, the troubles in Zimbabwe, and a mysterious death are all woven together in this intriguing narrative by this talented storyteller. The varied interests of a diverse cast of memorable characters are skillfully portrayed to make this an enjoyable read, but disturbing as well—the author's clear intention. *Barbara Flynn, former teacher*

Long a trusted bulwark in the crucial time of life of "babies to four's," a multicultural child development center swings its staff, parents, and children into action against a darkness creeping closer as time rushes on. The earnest director is the unlikely sleuth in this suspenseful story. *Helen Berg*

Crucial Time

happy reading!
Elspeth Benton

ELSPETH BENTON

iUniverse, Inc.
New York Bloomington

iUniverse books may be ordered through booksellers or by contacting:

iUniverse
1663 Liberty Drive
Bloomington, IN 47403
www.iuniverse.com
1-800-Authors (1-800-288-4677)

Because of the dynamic nature of the Internet, any Web addresses or links
contained in this book may have changed since publication and may no longer be
valid. The views expressed in this work are solely those of the author and do not
necessarily reflect the views of the publisher, and the publisher hereby disclaims
any responsibility for them.

ISBN: 978-1-4401-7533-6 (sc)
ISBN: 978-1-4401-7532-9 (ebook)
ISBN: 978-1-4401-7531-2 (hc)

Library of Congress Control Number: 2009911125

Printed in the United States of America

iUniverse rev. date: 11/5/2009

Shona names

Chipo: CHEEP-oh
Farai: FAR-eye
Ruvimbo: Roo-VIM-bow
Tapiwa: Tah-PEE-wah

Shona words

aiwa: alas
amai: mother
ambuya: grandmother
anopenga: she was crazy
baba: father
chibage: maize
Chibuku: popular alcoholic drink
chisurai: good-bye
Chimurenga: the 1896 rebellion against the British
danda: post
Mhondoro: the Shona spirit leader of the Chimurenga
mhoro: hello
midzumu: spirits of the ancestors
mukaka: milk
mupengo: rice
muriwo: leafy vegetable
mwanakomana: son
mwanasakana: daughter
Mwari: supreme deity
ndapata: honey
potsi, piri, tatu, ini, shona: numbers one through five
sadza: casava meal mush

Acknowledgment is gratefully made to the following:

First stanza of Emily Dickinson's *"There's a certain slant of light"* reprinted by permission of the publishers and the Trustees of Amherst College from THE POEMS OF EMILY DICKINSON, Thomas H. Johnson, ed., Cambridge, Mass.: The Belknap Press of Harvard University Press, Copyright 1951, 1955, 1979, 1983 by the President and Fellows of Harvard College
Farrar, Strauss and Giroux, LLC to mention *Angus and the Ducks*, by Marjorie Flack.
Fotolia, cover photograph
Green Street Café in Pasadena, CA; Bob Harrison
Sam Hinton, singer and guitarist, and his record, *Whoever Shall Have Some Good Peanuts*
LEGOS bricks
Lescher Ltd. to mention *The 10th Good Thing About Barney*, by Judith Viorst
Sleepytime Tea

for Laura

Pasadena, California
Wednesday, January 20, 1999

Careening toward the brightly lit pizza stand, the bicyclist scattered the line of waiting parents and children and smashed into the generator. Shards of glass exploded and tinkled in the sudden dark as he jammed on his brakes. He hurtled over the gravel into Tapiwa Moyo, who shielded his four-year-old son, Farai. The impact with concrete killed Tapiwa instantly. But at first, in the darkness, no one knew this. A moment earlier, Sue Bowles, a parent from the nearby Pasadena Child Development Center, was standing behind Tapiwa in the line, her eyes on the laughing boy looking up at his father. Now her senses filled with screams and cries.

She groped for the boy but encountered a sickening void. Farai Moyo was gone.

1

Pasadena Child Development Center
Tuesday, January 12, 1999

Angie's voice rose at the end of each sentence. "Something different about the way the gate opened in the dark, Hannah, but I couldn't see clearly enough to tell what it was? I think it was something about the sound of the latch? I noticed it, but didn't pay attention, know what I mean? I was planning how I'd use the time before six thirty to set up the room for the kids."

It was six in the morning in the four-year-olds' building at the Pasadena Child Development Center, and the center's director, Hannah Cooper, had arrived early for some quiet work time, but Angie called to her and she'd come right over. Sitting low on a child's chair, she looked up at Angie now, listening deeply, understanding her employee's need to release her agitation. A grandmother in her mid-fifties, Hannah had worked with young children and their families all her adult life. Lines ran from the corners of her mouth like backward quotation marks, etched by sadness as well as laughter. Beneath her short gray curls her alert, deep-set blue eyes looked out at her world.

She took in the sight of Angie leaning against the children's cubbies, her hands bracing her limp body, all her usual vibrancy drained by her need to talk. Though at fifty-five Angie was a few years older than Hannah, her hair was still a deep brown, and she wore it long and straggly. It emphasized her customary pallor, and today the pallor verged on green.

"Besides my set-up jobs like taking the kids' chairs off the tables and opening the shades—I open them first thing I come in, even when it's dark?—I had something else in mind. Like I said, I was planning something fresh for the kids—that's why I came in a little before six. That way I have a little more than half an hour."

Hannah opened her mouth to respond, but Angie continued without pause, her chatter streaming like a freeway with no on-ramps. Her voice was shrill and wobbly, and her words came so fast Hannah had to strain to pick them out.

"Some of the teachers think just a few crayons and some paper's enough? Of course when the kids first arrive, it's true they're usually still sleepy, they don't want much stimulation. They won't eat breakfast at *home* half the time. Heck, a lot of *parents* don't eat breakfast either! The kids aren't combed, sometimes they're still in their pj's—not ready for some huge super-activity—like, say, making pretzels from scratch—"

Angie laughed at the very idea, then bowed her head and closed her eyes, and Hannah knew she wished she could stay with this part of the story.

"Go on, Angie," she urged gently.

"Well, I guess I'm getting away from telling you what happened. I was trying to say that just the same old box of crayons and the same old recycled eight-and-a-half-by-eleven paper that parents bring from their offices—well, that's not enough. The kids deserve a little variety, a little imagination, and it helps them ease into their day too. Anyone should be able to see that.

"Not to badmouth anybody, but some of the teachers here just don't seem to get it? Maybe it's because I have kids of my own, I remember what it felt like to coax my own sleepy boys to wake up. Oh God, I wish I could have afforded to send them here instead of leaving them with my grandma ... but that's off the subject." She set her mouth into a resolute line.

Outside, rain was falling, muffling the sound of traffic on Del Monte Boulevard half a block away and creating a protected cave-like feeling around the two women talking in the dim, otherwise empty classroom.

"So I was focusing on something different for this early part of the morning, maybe those large leaves we collected on our walk yesterday?—I could put those out and the kids could draw around them, even cut out the shapes they made." Her voice continued to rise at the end of her sentences, as if pleading for Hannah to understand.

"I tell you Hannah, I get carried away with this kind of stuff! I can't believe you pay me to do it. It's so much *fun*. Oh, this was going to be so much better than just a few crayons and some old paper—"

"Please Angie," Hannah broke in at last, "tell me about the emergency. I want to help."

Angie took a breath. "Well ... I went out to the play yard to get the leaves from one of the outdoor cupboards where we stored them yesterday. It was a little lighter, the sky overcast?— and a wind came up, maybe the start of a Santa Ana. The kids love windy days, but they always make me feel anxious. My feelings come up, know what I mean?

"Please go on, dear. I want to know."

"I stepped around some puddles to get to the storage cupboard. My sneakers are old, so getting them muddy didn't matter, but I *had* hoped to keep them as dry as possible and not have to scrape them off before I went back in the building." She looked straight down into her director's eyes. Tears threatened, and her chest rose with a deep inhalation.

"Oh God, Hannah, my foot squished against something soft, and I felt so weird, like I had stepped on a big slug with bumps in it? When I looked down I saw footprints all around and this muddy, bloody, furry shape. Such a shock! It was Henry—you know Henry—one of our pet rabbits here in the four-year-olds' yard? The cage torn open, the door dangled on one hinge. Whoever did it didn't need to yank it like that—you know we don't padlock those cages. Mabel, the other rabbit, miserable in the back of the cage, shivering." Angie snuffled, rummaged in her pocket for a tissue, and blew her nose.

Then she raised her chin, looked straight at Hannah again, and said in a firmer tone, "I don't mind telling you, Hannah, I wanted to run. My whole world spun. In just one second, everything changed."

Hannah rose and held Angie close. "I'm so sorry this happened to you," she murmured in a shaky voice, close to tears herself. She remembered another child care center where almost the same thing had happened—rabbits and guinea pigs killed during the night. *What was it about innocent places that seemed to attract violence?*

"People can be twisted and do ugly things." She clicked her tongue. Then she released Angie and went outside to inspect the limp body next to the animal cages along the side of the children's play yard.

Angie joined her, handing her a box. They laid Henry in it on his side and adjusted his twisted little body so it appeared straight and relaxed. Pets died of natural causes at the center from time to time, and the staff response had been worked out years earlier. The children would be told that the animal had died and allowed to see and even stroke their pet's body—with supervised hand washing immediately afterward, of course. The regular group meetings of staff and children during this day would touch on Henry's death, and the children would be encouraged to say what they felt. At the end of the day, Hannah or one of the staff would take the body to the local Humane Society for disposal. For the next several days, even weeks, the children would mention Henry and staff would respond sympathetically and creatively.

Now Angie was standing taller. Her eyes shone as she mapped out for Hannah the new Henry-centered curriculum for the day. "Farai was especially fond of Henry," she told Hannah. "I'll need to keep an eye out for him. This will be hard for him. But with Farai ... I think I know something that will help." And she busied herself with pulling out supplies for a discussion and drawing session about Henry, and about all rabbits, later that morning.

"You know, Angie," Hannah said, "I was wondering if you were up to being with the kids this morning, but it looks as if you're together again—and thinking of their needs as usual. You are one strong lady!" She hugged Angie again, feeling her own tears welling. "But watch yourself, my dear. If you feel wobbly, I want you to go home for a hot bath, and we'll get a substitute for your group. Agreed?"

"I'll be okay, Hannah. I know I will."

Hannah herself experienced a renewed surge of strength. This work could break her heart and make her feel such joy and hope for the human race, all in the same moment sometimes.

But Angie had been right earlier. Everything *had* changed. When a pet rabbit is slain in the night outside its own cage, it's the opposite of sharing, the opposite of taking turns, the opposite of talking things through. Their little world of trust-building had been violated. It felt like a terrible intrusion into what should be the safest of all worlds.

Eleven hours later, the parents had picked up the last of their children. As Hannah tidied the children's cubbies, she could clearly hear Angie's voice on the phone across the room. Angie gave her a wave and continued talking. "So that's what happened, Mom. Awful, but we got through it. The kids wanted me to get a padlock for Mabel's cage, so after my shift I went and got one. I came back and ...

"Yes it *was* on my own time, but sometimes you just have to do what you have to do, Ma, you know that. We'll all sleep better tonight with that padlock on Mabel's cage ...

"It'll be hard to go into the yard tomorrow, though, I'll tell you. Kathy said she'd come early so I wouldn't be by myself ... What?

"I *know* you don't understand why I chose this work, and I *know* you think I have a problem here, that I'm addicted to children or something ... Aw, Ma, I know it's a worry to you, no retirement benefits and all, but I'll be okay when I reach sixty-five, honest I will. I'll figure it out. I just love my work—it's that simple. That's worth something, now, isn't it? ...

"Ma, you're the best. I always feel better when I talk to you."

2

Harare, Zimbabwe
August 1998

"*Amai,* Farai's had an earache all night. I have to be at work. They won't let me take any more sick time now because we're leaving so soon, and Tapiwa has to go alone to the passport office today. Can you—"

Over the static of her cell phone, Ruvimbo heard the anxiety in her daughter Chipo's voice.

"I'm sorry he's hurting, *mwanasikana,*" she responded. "It's these dry August winds—they're so bad for the ears. But I'm free and willing, so just bring him along! Do you have willow extract?"

"No, *Amai.* I don't have those old recipes you used with me. I've been giving him children's Tylenol every three hours. I'll bring some along. Anyway, I have him scheduled at the clinic at eleven thirty. Can I drop him off with you now and—"

"You want me to take him to a doctor? I know what to do for earache, *mwanasikana.* Remember when you—"

"I really don't have time to reminisce now, *Amai.* I want you to take Farai to the clinic at eleven thirty, and get them to look at his ear. They'll give him antibiotic if he needs it."

Ruvimbo would never have spoken to her own mother in such a disrespectful way, even if behind her mother's back she might have criticized her. She sank onto the wooden stool at her table and closed her eyes tight, pulling her lips together. Why had she not been able to raise her daughter to treat her with more formal respect?

Chipo continued, her voice suddenly teary, "Mother, I do appreciate how you've helped me with Farai when I've been in a jam, and I need you to help me today."

"Of course, dear, I'll try to do what you say. See you in a little bit." Ruvimbo tried to keep her voice warm, not tight with the hurt she felt, and turned off the phone. She tugged at the tight waves of her thick gray hair as she stood in thought for a moment.

Catching her reflection in the small cracked mirror by her door, she adjusted her red robe and nodded with satisfaction at the way it glowed in the early morning light against her glossy, dark brown skin. Her daughter might think her mother's time was over, but as Ruvimbo gazed at the sturdy woman in the mirror, she took note of her shapely arms. Her lips curved upward in an approving smile. No, she was not to be put away like an old garment. Not yet. She had much to offer the world. Much to offer her daughter and grandson too.

She looked around her old cottage, a one-room cabin built as a servant shelter by the colonials. Her cell phone, one electric light with plug-in outlet, and indoor plumbing had been added later and were her only modern conveniences. It didn't feel much different to her from the round hut with thatched roof she'd inhabited in the village where she'd grown up.

She put aside her weaving project, a blanket for little Farai, and let her thoughts wander. Best to cover the loom when a four-year-old comes to visit, even a sick one, she knew. Farai was always on the move, curious and active. She smiled, picturing him playing with her pots and pans, digging in her vegetable plot, investigating her weaving yarns, pulling Coomi's tail when he thought his grandmother wasn't looking.

Coomi growled faintly. The old dog stretched slowly to his feet, brown ears and tail stiff and alert.

"*Muriwo! Mukaka! Mupenga!*"

Her friend Tatenda the peddler ambled down the road in front of her cabin, singing his goods and wares.

"Coomi, it's just Tatenda," she reassured her skinny companion. "You know he comes by here every morning. But I'm glad you growl. You're my reliable warning system, that's what you are. It's all I can do to feed you, but you're worth every mouthful." She and Coomi had been together for a long time—over twelve years. She reached down and scratched gently between his ears, and he returned the love with a melting, brown-eyed gaze.

Since Farai would be coming, Ruvimbo wanted some of Tatenda's fresh goat milk. She always had food growing, even at this colder time of the year: okra, *muriwo*, onions, groundnuts, *chibage*. Sometimes she could sell her vegetables at the *musica* for money, but with Tatenda she bartered as they had in the village where she grew up. She stepped into her sandals, pulled aside the heavy double burlap curtain that served as her door during this chilly season, and hurried out to negotiate with Tatenda.

She noticed that her agile step drew his appreciative gaze, which lingered on her ankles and the motion of her hips as she walked toward him. He brought his slow-moving motorized cart to a halt. Tatenda's father before him had been a peddler, and he felt comfortable in his role of bearing varied foods and other goods, exchanging gossip, and generally being part of the glue holding together this Mbare neighborhood on the southern outskirts of Harare. He was a slight man, stooped, his wispy hair white, his skin sallow. His hawk eyes surveyed all that he passed each day and rarely missed a detail, either obvious or subtle. He and Ruvimbo were old friends of the same generation; they'd lived through more changes than they themselves could begin to describe. They exchanged warm smiles as she held out her empty cup and asked him to fill it with *mukaka*.

"And what might you give me in return?" he asked her, his head cocked to one side and his gaze enveloping her.

She ignored the implied meaning of his question, "I have some fresh turnips I can pull for you if you like."

With a roll of his eyes, he left his cart and accompanied her to her doorway, where he waited while she entered and set down the milk on her table. Then he walked with her to the vegetable plot at the side of her cottage and watched as she knelt and pulled up three medium-sized turnips.

"Will these be enough?" The leaves shone, crisp and green.

"Your vegetables are always tasty, Ruvimbo," he told her. "I hope no one wants to buy them from me today, because they will make me a wonderful soup this evening."

He walked back with her to his cart and asked, "And how is your little rascal?"

"Meaning Coomi or Farai?" she joked.

"Farai, to be sure. That little sprout is growing taller, isn't he? Will he go to school soon?"

"He'll enter primary school in a year or so," she told him, omitting the fact that this would take place in California rather than in Harare. To share the news of Tapiwa's good fortune, even with a trusted friend like Tatenda, would not be wise. Jealousy and suspicion could cause serious trouble for her son-in-law.

"I have heard that Tapiwa may leave us?" he pushed.

"Ah, you would have to ask him about that," she responded, stooping to remove some mud from her sandal. "I expect a visit from Farai this morning. He'll enjoy your good milk, I know."

"Well then, I'll see you tomorrow, Ruvimbo. Just remember, though, if you should need anything, I am your friend and I would want to offer any assistance I could."

She dropped her eyes. "It is an ugly time in our country, Tatenda, and often I worry about this. So it is good to have friends. And I thank you. I will remember."

The exchange completed, Tatenda ambled back to the street. Back in her cabin, Ruvimbo put the milk in her cold cupboard, a ventilated box on the shaded side of her cabin. She felt a warm anticipation of Farai's arrival any moment now.

Coomi growled and ran to the door, and Ruvimbo roused from her thoughts and met Chipo with Farai in her arms. She wore a long, full, blue skirt, clingy green short-sleeved top, and sandals with low heels. Ruvimbo felt sure, though she'd never been there, that in New York City Chipo could have blended in as well as here in Harare. She was struck, not for the first time, by her daughter's beauty. At twenty-eight, Chipo stood tall and slender, taller even than her mother, with masses of thick hair pinned at the back of her head and graceful carriage. Her clear, almost stern look pierced her mother's heart as she stepped into the cabin. Then, with a vestige of the respect Ruvimbo had tried to instill in her, Chipo bent her knees slightly in a token curtsey, made awkward by holding Farai. The almost imperceptible gesture lasted less than a second.

"Chipo, how pretty you look. Your father would be so proud—"

"He didn't get much sleep last night, *Amai*," Chipo cut through her mother's compliment. "Mostly he was awake with the pain. He seems easier now with the Tylenol. Maybe he'll sleep. Put him on your bed, tuck him in, and let him rest until you leave for the clinic. It's right nearby." Chipo's anxiety sharpened her tone.

Wrapped in a large shawl and weighing perhaps forty pounds, Farai was handed over to his grandmother. His body felt tense to her, and she noted the pale skin below his eyes.

"I know where the clinic is. Has he eaten anything since last night?" Ruvimbo asked as patiently as she could.

"Just a little water. Here's the Tylenol. He had some at six thirty this morning, so give him some more at nine thirty, and take it with you to the clinic at eleven thirty to show them, okay? Call me at work if you need to." She handed her mother a few bills. "Here's something to pay for antibiotic if he needs it. I have to run, *Amai*. See you this afternoon." And with this, Chipo rushed off to her job at the Ministry of Vital Statistics.

Farai looked into his grandmother's eyes. His thin body relaxed, his eyes closed, and before she could lay him on her bed, he fell deeply asleep. She sat close to him, gently stroking his head and back. She kissed his toes, "*Potsi, piri, tatu, ini, shona* ... Farai, my little Farai, you're going to feel well again! Soon you'll be all rested and ready to play with Coomi—he's waiting for you now!"

She sat with Farai like that for some time, then rose, tiptoed to her kerosene stove, took some herbs from her small supply, and brewed an aromatic tea. Farai woke. His grandmother brought a small cup of the steaming tea to him, lightly braced his body upright against hers with her left arm, and brought the cup a few inches from his lips with her right hand. "Ugh! *Ambuya*, I know this stuff! It tastes bad!" said Farai, screwing up his face and turning down the corners of his mouth.

"Well, I'm glad you remember it!" said Ruvimbo. She set the tea down and rocked him gently as she spoke. "So then maybe you also remember how this good tea made you all better last time you were here, and you and Coomi were able to play!" Then she lifted the tea to her own lips and took a sip. It tasted of mint and lemon. "Mmmmm!"

"Okay, *Ambuya*, but only one little sip," Farai consented, taking a minuscule taste of the fragrant brew. He followed this with one or two swallows more to satisfy his thirst.

"*Ambuya*, do you have any of that good *sadza*?"

Ruvimbo smiled a whole smile. She got up from the bed, went to her cold cupboard, and took the goat milk to the stove, where she warmed it. Then she mixed a small portion of cassava meal with the milk, the way Farai liked it. Pungent goat essence filled the dim little room, and Coomi's tail thumped expectantly. Ruvimbo sat beside her grandson and wiped both his hands, finger by finger, with a clean, damp cloth, and offered him a spoonful of *sadza*. But he wanted to feed himself and took the small bowl to her table, where he could do this more easily. At the table he saw a bowl of *muriwo*—chopped greens fried with onions and tomatoes. He gathered a walnut-sized bit of *sadza* in one hand and wrapped up the *muriwo* in a wiping gesture. When he'd finished, she kissed his forehead carefully, feeling his temperature with her lips. His skin felt slightly warm, but no more than her own. She wiped Farai's hands again with the cloth and placed his almost empty bowl on the floor for Coomi.

"Farai, I believe you're getting better." Gently, she touched the base of his left ear. "*Amai* said this hurt last night. Do you remember?"

"It was bad, *Ambuya*, but now it feels okay," he declared in a loud, happy voice. He smiled and rubbed both ears vigorously to back up his words. Ruvimbo smiled too. Farai always made her happy. She could hardly bear it that he and his parents would leave in a couple of weeks for the United States. She was proud that he could speak so well. She loved everything about him—the way he half-skipped when he walked, his habit of cocking his head to one side when you spoke to him, his curiosity about new sounds and objects. As an infant he had opened his eyes and listened intently to a bird singing, or Coomi growling, or Tatenda's morning street calls. If you put a leaf, a stone, or a feather into his hand, he'd turn it round and round, rub his fingers over it, even taste it—you had to watch him every minute, make sure the stone was clean and too large to swallow, that the leaf was not poisonous. *I'm more experienced now than when Chipo was little, and I can truly enjoy my grandson's company!* She smiled at herself. The phone rang sharply, rousing her from this pleasant reverie. *"Amai,* what did they tell you at the clinic?" came Chipo's urgent voice.

3

Hannah heard quick steps on the stairs outside her office seconds before Joan Nefas strode in, breathless and urgent. At five foot ten, Joan was small boned and so thin as almost to appear emaciated. Fifty-three years old, she'd worked at the center since 1982. She wore a dark brown pantsuit—brown and black were her customary colors. Her long hair hung thick and dark, creating for Hannah the overall impression of the postmistress/wicked witch in the *Wizard of Oz*. Her green eyes darted rapidly from Hannah to Gina, the bookkeeper, and a hectic flush burned on her cheeks. For Hannah, need for food and rest was on her mind that afternoon. She tried not to think how Joan's unannounced arrival, interrupting her composing the board report, would mean either postponing her dinner or returning to her office in the evening to complete the report. Hannah took her health seriously, eating sensibly and exercising daily. She wanted to postpone aging as long as she could.

"I'm wondering if you'd be willing—I think it might be

necessary, something we all need after this terrible rabbit killing, if you could arrange to have a healer come and exorcise our play yards." Joan's gentle tone contrasted with the sharp look she cast at her boss. Her pupils appeared dilated, and Hannah noted a slight tremor in her hands.

She's so earnest. She has those deeply intuitive feelings you need to work with young children, but in her, the feelings run amok. She seems to want to enlarge her fears, not keep them in perspective.

"You see," Joan continued, "all of us are terribly affected by the killing—staff and parents too. We can hardly function. An exorcism might help get us back on track." She breathed heavily, wiped her brow, and gave Hannah an urgent look, tears clearly imminent.

"Joan, I wonder if we're possibly making too much out of this." Hannah used "we" instead of "you" to soften her words, but with an inner groan.

"Don't you feel the actions we've already taken are enough? We've padlocked the rabbit cage, stepped up campus security, called a meeting, and arranged for the sheriff to talk with parents, and then there's Phyllis, the mom in Anne's class who's a therapist. And you and your fours staff have done a great job with the children about this as well."

Joan's mouth tightened in anger and habitual disappointment. Once again, the director was failing her and the entire center with her limited ability to understand the feelings of those she was supposed to serve.

"Well, it was just an idea." She sighed, jumped to her feet, and began pacing between Gina's desk and Hannah's. "I thought you probably wouldn't approve it." She turned and raced out of the office without another word.

"She's not hap-py," Gina sang from her desk, where she was quietly putting paychecks into envelopes. She had stayed later than usual to complete this task. In her twenties and recently married, Gina provided a steady objectivity about the center's thirty-five staff members, without feeling a need to delve deeply into their psyches or form intense relationships with them outside of work. Energetic and pretty, she maintained her fitness by using PTI's gym on her lunch hour, and hiking on weekends.

"Of course it's horrible that anyone would kill one of our pets, but she's not helping by trying to put blame on you for not doing more about it."

"Oh well, Gina," Hannah said in as mild a tone as she could muster. "She's just upset that anyone would do something so ugly."

Really upset, thought Hannah, *and doing everything she can to get herself more upset and whip up the staff's anxiety and fears as well. Damn all these unnecessary histrionics! Yes, killing a pet's ugly! Of course it's scary! But can't we act strong, neutralize the damage, and model courage? Why make things worse?*

"It's funny," she said aloud, "Joan's so calm when we have mishaps like an earthquake. And remember the Rodney King riots when we could smell the smoke in our play yards, how she soothed children and parents? But certain things just set her off, like this rabbit killing or if one of the teachers has a personal sadness. Then Joan loses all perspective and joins forces with whoever's scared or angry and encourages all their negative feelings."

"I know. It's weird when you think about it, isn't it?" Gina put down her paychecks for a moment while she considered Joan's actions. "She seems to want to make people's sad feelings worse than they already are! And to get us *all* stuck in them! What do you think causes it?"

"Oh, it's the old story. So many things make it hard for her and for all of us—low wages for starters. Not one of us on this staff actually makes a living wage. But then again, no one *made* us go into this kind of work." Hannah broke off her musing, knowing her words might be repeated and exaggerated, even by Gina, whom she trusted. "Well, back to the board report.

Oops, it's five fifteen already!" At this time of day, Hannah needed to be available to parents picking up their children, either downstairs or in one of the other center buildings. She tried to rotate buildings each evening. She left her desk awash with graphs and charts and hurried out.

❦   ❦   ❦

About 8:30 that evening the laser printer consented to make fifteen copies of the completed board report, and then with a groan its light went out and silence ensued. Hannah's groan echoed the printer's. She crawled behind the machine and disconnected it, to take it once again the next day to the Computer Shack for attention. She wound the cord around it, hoisted it to her right hip, placed the office key between her teeth, slung her purse over her shoulder, took the agendas in her free hand, switched off the lights with her elbow, and closed the office door. She set everything on the floor in the hall outside the office, locked the door, and put the key safely in her purse. Then she picked up her load, descended the stairs, and placed the broken printer on top of the children's cubbies in the threes room.

I hate closing, she thought. *It's really the downside of my work.*

She kicked one of the cubbies just hard enough to feel the blow on the top of her foot and felt a little better. Then she tucked the board agendas into Board President Andrew Chin's mailbox, retrieved the printer, went out the back door, locked it, and headed for her car.

It would feel good to get home, she knew. It would be a return to her own personal core, and after this long, challenging day, she needed to recharge.

4

Pasadena
Thursday, January 14

"So what are you up to this week, Hannah?" Mary Weiss sipped her coffee and assumed an expectant listening pose, her brown eyes eager. "They're never dull, the stories you tell me!" Hannah and Mary were enjoying an early breakfast at the Green Street Café as they usually did on Thursdays. The two friends had tried many Pasadena coffee shops, but "Green," as they affectionately called it, remained their favorite, even though the first cup of coffee tended to be lukewarm. Green opened at six in the morning, for starters. Two dollars would get you an oatmeal-and-raisin breakfast—serious nutrition for the strenuous days Hannah and Mary faced in their respective workplaces. Coffee was replenished magically; the servers knew how to take care of you without interrupting. Variable art exhibits enlivened the walls, and interesting people were often at nearby tables, some of them well known from City Hall. Altogether a pleasant place to begin the day.

Mary Weiss headed the personnel department in a large

cosmetic firm in Highland Park, southwest of Pasadena. The two women had been good friends for the better part of two decades.

"I've been thinking of you ever since you called me Tuesday. Now, tell me what you've done about this bunny incident. Still no clue as to who did it?" Mary asked Hannah without waiting for someone to take their orders. She settled back to listen.

"None whatsoever, and both the campus police and the sheriff's office have investigated. They have the name of a homeless man discovered asleep in the play yard one night last fall, but no way of finding and checking him out. They think maybe a hungry homeless person might have killed this poor rabbit for food, was interrupted by the nightly campus security check, and just dropped it, climbed the fence, and disappeared."

Their server, who knew them both as regulars, appeared and took their usual orders. "I've tried everything I can think of to counteract the scariness of it. Our first thought was for the children, of course. Joan and her staff had a discussion with their group of fours—"

"What are 'fours'?" Mary cut off her friend.

"Come on, Mary, duh! 'Fours' are four-year-olds, of *course!*" Hannah paused as Mary rolled her eyes. "Anyway, Joan and her staff had a discussion with their group of *four year olds*"—she smiled at Mary—"the morning it happened, and out of that came a little 'good-bye Henry' time they planned together."

"Does every yard have live pets?"

"Yes."

"Hannah, whoever did this might return. Even if campus security checks the yards nightly, or says it does, shouldn't you consider padlocking all the yards, and the rabbit pens as well?"

Hannah seemed not to hear Mary's concern as she continued. "For the adults, I've taken even more measures. I got out a bulletin to all the teachers and parents the same day, telling them the facts and inviting them to a panel to talk about security. Oh—and we did do the padlock thing, gates *and* animal pens. Of course we don't *like* using padlocks. Padlocks represent the opposite of the trust we try to model and build. But for now, it seems more important to reassure the children this way," Hannah's voice trailed regretfully as their server placed steaming bowls of oatmeal before them.

Mary listened intently to her friend. She loved Hannah's idealism, but sometimes feared for her as well. Hannah was grounded in early childhood development theory and possessed of incredible generosity and heart, but Mary noted that sometimes her friend was unaware of how adults might receive her actions. "Has this calmed Joan at all?"

"No, nothing seems to lessen her fears or stop her encouraging other staff to be terrified. But maybe I *have* succeeded in making an end run around her and reassuring and calming the parents and the other teachers. I really hope so." Hannah subsided, looking down at her untouched breakfast.

"I don't see a thing more that anyone could do, Hannah. Looks like you'll just have to batten the hatches and ride out the storm."

Hannah shifted gears. "Okay Mary, let me switch from this gloom and tell you something wonderful in my life. It might sound dull to most people, but it excites me."

Mary moved her empty bowl and settled back in anticipation. "Exciting! All right, let's hear about it!"

"It's the EC seminar in administration I'm taking at UCLA on Saturdays. I have two—"

"Hold on, Hannah. You and your acronyms! What's 'EC'?"

"EC? It's extracurricular, of course!" Hannah waited for Mary's laugh, but her friend's face retained its puzzled look. "I'm sorry, Mary. EC means Early Childhood, short for Early Childhood Education, okay?"

"Okay, go on then," Mary encouraged.

"I have two assignments for this EC class, to observe and record children's groups at my own center. The teacher encourages us to include background information and our thoughts, sort of stream of consciousness."

Mary shifted both elbows onto the table, leaned forward, squeezed her face between her hands, and stabbed the air with one index finger. "Let me get this straight. You're *excited* about driving all the way to West Los Angeles and back on your Saturdays, just for a class?" She glanced sideways at her friend.

Hannah nodded slowly twice, her chin touching her chest, eyes closed and mouth drawn into a tight line.

"Hmmm. What ages will you observe? "

"Probably just the fours. We have two four-year-old classes, you know."

"What will *you* get out of this, Hannah?"

"A better understanding of the dynamics in our two fours classes is what I'm hoping for. One feels comfortable and bursting with creativity and general joy, and the other just seems to plod along."

"Hmmm. Let me guess which one's Joan's group." Mary glanced at her watch. "This hour went too fast. Hannah, would you be able to breakfast here with me again tomorrow, same time? I have a couple more questions I want to ask you."

She looked concerned, and Hannah agreed, grateful for the support. Then she brightened and announced, "I think I've figured out why our first cup of coffee's never hot. It's the cups! The cups are cold in the morning."

But Hannah felt warmed now, and ready to face her day. *Thanks, Mary.*

5

Harare
August 1998

"So here they are at last, young man!" the woman at the Harare Immigration Control Office told Tapiwa Moyo. A broad smile lit up her wrinkled face as she showed him the two slim brown passports—one for him, and one for his wife Chipo and their four-year-old son Farai. Tapiwa noticed the tremble of the woman's hands, and that her head shook too. *With sixty percent unemployment, how had the old woman gotten this job? She must be the mother of someone powerful, maybe a policeman.*

The end of the morning neared, and at noon the office would close for a three-hour-or-longer afternoon siesta. Tapiwa felt relieved to have made it here in time.

"Just make sure you do come back in two years, in September of two thousand, the way these papers say," she told him sternly. She opened his passport, unfolded a stamped document affixed to the inside front cover, and slowly, with great seriousness, read him a short paragraph with which they were both already completely familiar:

> The bearer of this passport is permitted to leave his native country for two years of study only. The Government of Zimbabwe requires that he return at the end of that time, no later than September first, 2000, and that he be available to the Zimbabwean Government for two years after his return.

"What is it that you're going to America to study?" she asked him.

"Engineering, ma'am." He spoke respectfully, as was his way with elders. Part of him would have liked to tell her his dreams of building bridges, roads, and houses on his return, but he well knew that his departure caused jealousy in most who learned of it. So, least said, the better. This visa and scholarship were miracles stemming from his late father having been a chief. The name Tendekai Moyo still carried weight here.

Six foot four in height, lean, with intelligent eyes and white teeth flashing in his dark face, Tapiwa won the woman's interest, and she tried to keep him at her desk a little longer. She glanced around the room and spoke in a low voice. "With the unrest in our country, some seek to leave for good," she said. "Are you one of these?" She spoke in the clipped British way.

Of course, Tapiwa did not say that he thought the present government, headed by Robert Mugabe, was leading its people to ruin. He did not add that he and many of his friends hoped to overthrow this leader soon and create a more constructive government, one that had compassion for its people as its cornerstone. Instead, he shook his head sideways. "No, ma'am, this is my country." Reassured, she held the passports out to him and asked, "When will you depart?"

"Our flight is arranged for two weeks from today," he told her. He gave three soft claps in gratitude and accepted the passports.

"May your trip, and your stay abroad, be all that you desire," she told him, "and may you return safe to this native land that you love."

A strong, intuitive voice told her that things could be difficult for this young prince. She wanted to embrace him as an elder would have done in the former days, but since she didn't know him, not even as a distant cousin or nephew, she abided by the new ways and simply offered him her right hand across the desk, placing her left hand on her right arm as she did so. He understood her care for him, and took her hand and shook it as he looked into her eyes.

"May things be well with you also," he said.

6

Harare
August 1998

Dear Sekai,

Your old friend Ruvimbo here!

When I last heard from you, you were thinking of moving to a nearby area with less expensive housing, but you sounded cheerful. I'm glad you don't miss your husband as badly as you did just after his death. My heart ached for you when Steve died, and you alone in a strange country—though maybe it doesn't feel so strange after eighteen years. If I could have scraped up the money at that time, I would have come and visited you.

You know, it seems only day before yesterday that we were in high school together, trying to learn English, cramming for finals, doing each other's hair, playing hooky sometimes! So much has happened in the last three decades, yet I still feel our closeness, old friend. I know you remember how bad those times got. Armed thugs everywhere, no food. Enough about that!

But I have to say, when I look back on it now, it's clear to see that Ian Smith *encouraged* the Ndebele uprisings and Shona repressions. Anyway, as you know, it was under his regime that my husband Tinashe, a Ndebele, was taken from our home to die in prison. If I hadn't had Chipo to care for, I think I would have let myself die as well. She was my blessing. It was for her I kept going, for her I found food. And then, you remember after Mugabe took over, she and I were assigned the cabin where you visited me just before you and Steve left for the States. I could earn a little money for Chipo to have schooling, and at that time there were even scholarships for her to go to college.

Now here comes the surprise. You won't believe it, perhaps, but my dear Chipo, her husband Tapiwa, and their little Farai are actually coming to America! And not just America but Pasadena! Tapiwa has a graduate fellowship in civil engineering at the Pasadena Technological Institute—PTI, they call it. I'm so happy for them, though I'll miss them terribly—I don't have to tell you. They'll be safer in California than here too.

About Chipo, as I've written you before, she's no longer warm to me. I always hope we'll be close again some day, but right now I can only sadly describe our relationship as one of near estrangement. The feminism she took up in university was so militant. I don't understand why new, enlightened movements so often become shrill and judgmental. You know how hard I worked for her to go to college. But now she judges me, finds me seriously lacking, because I still follow some of the old ways. Especially after Farai's birth in '94, she didn't want me to sing him our old Shona songs and chants, rock him to sleep in my arms, feed him the *sadza* and goat milk we were raised on, doctor him with the old herbal remedies. She sends him most days to a woman who looks after children in her home. I usually only see him on days when he can't go to that woman because of a cold or cough or fever.

She's still civil to me, but only barely, and things are so chilly between us, I can't express to you. It's probably just as well she'll be in America for a while; maybe she'll miss me just a little in California and be glad to see me when she comes back! Because it's definite they will come back: Tapiwa's fellowship is from the government, and he has it only on condition of returning and working for at least two years in the Transportation Department here in Zimbabwe. Lord knows, Zimbabwe needs him. Our few roads—and our whole country—are falling apart.

Anyway, dear friend, once I know where they set up housekeeping in Pasadena—if Chipo lets me know her address —I'll send it to you, and possibly, if it feels right to you, you might stop in to see her. She may not remember you, since she was only a baby when you visited. But I talked to her about you when she was growing up, and I know she admires you for moving and adapting to a new country (and so do I, my dear).

Hoping you are well and sending you love,

Ruvimbo

7

Tapiwa left the Immigration Control office and turned west on Nelson Mandela Avenue, then south on Angwa Street to walk the several miles to his apartment in the Mbare section of Harare. Buses were available, and he had many things to do in the two weeks before his departure, but he felt a need to walk. In moments he reached a quick stride, the rhythm of his feet on the concrete clearing his mind. He had the passports! An important task had been completed. He scarcely saw the sidewalk vendors' colorful wares or the many people sauntering toward him or passing him, sharing his path.

Rapid footsteps sounded behind him, and he half-turned, but before he could see his pursuers a blindfold snapped over his eyes and strong arms held him and dragged him into an opening on his right. Strong hands bit into his upper arms and led him down what felt like a narrow passageway. His clammy skin felt no currents of air; silence thickened around him. Then a left turn. Air brushed his cheeks—this must be a larger space.

He felt rather than heard a deep male voice commanding him to be quiet and sit down. He did so, and the blindfold was whipped off. In the half-light of the room, he discerned three masked figures, holes where their mouths and eyes should be. Two were slender and tall like himself while the third appeared shorter, perhaps five foot seven, and fat. The shorter man began the interview.

"We mean you no harm, Tapiwa, unless we find that you mean us harm," he began, forcefully, in the Shona tongue. "Do not speak except to answer our questions." Tapiwa nodded: he understood. He wanted to struggle and shout, but he had friends who had "disappeared" recently. With an effort, he postponed struggling and shouting for the moment. His captors had been forceful in taking him here, but as yet they had not harmed him.

"We know, of course, that you are preparing to leave Zimbabwe for the next two years, and that you mean to leave the Harare airport two weeks from today with your wife and son. We know about the study grant you have at the Pasadena Technological Institute in California and about the requirement that you return here in September, two thousand."

Tapiwa listened and waited as he'd been ordered to do.

"What we don't know is whether you're loyal to the government of your country," the heavyset man continued. "Do you plan to defect?"

Tapiwa started; it was the same very direct question the woman at Immigration Control had asked—more politely—not a quarter of an hour ago. The man paused for his response.

"No, I have no such plans. I wish only to gain skills so that I may serve my country." He wanted to add the polite "my elder" at the end of his response. It would indicate his respect, as a younger man, for his interrogator, but he knew this was not a typical interview. This interview was new, uncharted territory.

And this elder was not behaving well toward him. He had heard of such things from his friends, but actually being treated this way himself by an older countryman disturbed and deeply confused him.

"Very good. You will return to Zimbabwe in the year two thousand as agreed, then. We are glad to hear this." The man said these words with emphasis on each one. Then he continued, "And what about some of your friends here? We have intercepted some of your communications, and we question their loyalty to the present government."

Again Tapiwa waited.

"Some of your friends,"—the fat man mentioned two of the three who had disappeared in the last month—"have been found disloyal and are being detained in a safe place, where they can no longer communicate with their friends and families while they are further investigated. We would not like to have to carry out these same measures with you. Do you understand my meaning?"

Tapiwa nodded.

"Then we have no further business with you at this time. Know that during your absence we will be aware of all that you do. Go then, and return safely and in loyalty to your country." The man rose ponderously and signaled to the two youths.

Tapiwa winced as the blindfold once more bit into his skull. Again his arms were gripped as in a vise, and he was jerked from the room, then along the passageway. The three then descended some steps to what felt like an underground area—under the blindfold Tapiwa could see nothing. He tried to identify the smells that spoke loudly to him: human feces, he thought, and mold and decayed rags. His captors spoke neither to him nor to each other. After several turns, they mounted some steps, the blindfold was flung off again, and he was shoved into brilliant sunlight on a side road leading back toward Angwa Street.

8

Tapiwa wheeled around, but saw only a doorway behind a small empty clearing between two shops. The street itself pullulated with people, but he saw no one behind him. The sun's position indicated early afternoon, which amazed him. Had he dreamed the whole detainment? He looked at his arms, legs, feet. The upper arms bore ugly red marks, but he felt no bruises or scratches. He patted his inner shirt and felt the passports lodged in his pocket, safe.

Apparently the whole frightening experience was meant to be exactly that and only that: frightening. He would be allowed to leave Zimbabwe with his family, and he was to know beyond any doubt that he must return after his two years away.

Although he discounted the older man's threat of surveillance in California, his body shook and sweat prickled under his arms, seeped down his thighs. It would be a huge relief to head now to the apartment of one of his politically active friends and spill out to sympathetic ears what had just happened to him. He nearly turned his feet in that direction, but then his wily survivor self spoke to him, telling him not to compromise his friends but to instead head home to Chipo. Though he could see no one following him, he judged he'd been carefully tracked less than an hour ago, and in all likelihood someone watched him now too. He would be wary. He would be wise. He would go straight home.

As in a dream, he shuffled along narrow sidewalks close to busy streets, his head bowed as he relived what had just happened. Without conscious thought, he dodged small children and indignant mothers, skirted around sidewalk displays of fabrics, jewelry, vegetables. It surprised him when his four-story Western-style apartment building came into view. Had he really come this far? It seemed only a moment since he'd been shoved onto the street.

He entered the dark hallway, unlocked the inner door, and climbed the stairs to the small apartment he shared with Chipo and Farai. Again he unlocked a door; he had not grown up with doors, or locks, but that world was gone forever. He sank onto their bed. His pulse raced as he tried to think.

It would be good to see his boy. He hoped that, after the day with his grandmother, Farai would be better. He looked forward to a dinner cooked by Chipo; she cooked well. She had a good mind too. Sometimes it annoyed him to have a wife with such a good mind, but there were advantages to it too, he realized, and she would help him understand what had happened, and what—if anything—to do about it.

He looked around the simple room, three and a half by seven meters, they called an apartment. Furnished with a three-quarter-sized bed just wide enough for two, it also contained a table and three stools and a set of two shelves that held a few of his and Chipo's texts from the university. During the day Chipo tucked Farai's pallet under the bed. In one corner of the room was a sink with a cold water faucet, and next to that a shelf. A two-burner electric stove stood at the adjoining wall of this corner, and a shelf that held a few dishes and cooking pans ran beneath sink and stove. In this room they cooked, ate, occasionally entertained, and slept. They shared a bathroom down the hall with two other families.

Yet this apartment represented a big step up in standard of living compared to the simple, almost primitive conditions he'd been used to in his village as a boy. Though his father was a chief, he and his family slept on a mat on the ground inside his small, round hut, and his father's wives daily pounded grain for the evening staple, *sadza*. Tapiwa wanted a better home when he returned with his foreign degree, though he knew that most families in his country lived as he did or even less well. With wise government, the rich resources of Zimbabwe could result in prosperity for all, and he yearned to help make it happen. It was his country, his land.

He would die rather than let Mugabe ruin it!

The sound of voices interrupted his thoughts. At first he couldn't distinguish the words. Chipo appeared to be urging Farai up the stairs to their home, and Farai appeared to be dragging behind. *Probably to look at some ants or a spider web,* Tapiwa thought affectionately; his son took great interest in all that he saw. Chipo often complained about the lack of an elevator to their third-floor apartment—having to carry all their food upstairs, their husks and egg shells and such downstairs—but the boy relished the chance to explore the sights as he climbed or descended.

Chipo seemed always in a hurry now, Tapiwa mused, no longer the gentle young woman he had courted and married almost six years ago. His friends had warned him even then— "That woman, she has her own ideas, man! Too much school! Watch out for her! She's four years older than you; she'll try to boss you around"—and they'd shaken their heads with heavy portent.

But she'd been a pretty good wife, after all. She'd borne him a strong, healthy son, and she even brought in money with her Ministry of Vital Statistics job. He knew she was faithful to him, and she hadn't gotten fat like a lot of her friends either. Fat women had been considered beautiful when he was a child, but as a man, he liked Chipo's Western TV–style slenderness.

And her mother, Ruvimbo, didn't try to tell him what to do. He wished he'd known Chipo's father, Tinashe. They could have talked politics as he used to do with his own father before his death. He felt sure he could have learned much wisdom from his father-in-law, who'd died in jail as a political prisoner.

He heard the light sound of Chipo's sandals dropping to the floor outside the door, then a more emphatic sound as Farai slapped down his plastic zoris next to his mother's. That Farai walked rather than being carried by Chipo told Tapiwa that the boy's ear must be better. He sat up on the bed, swung his feet to the floor, and smiled as they entered the room.

Chipo went directly to the stove with her groceries; it was not the custom to kiss one's husband in front of a child. Farai flew to his father and knelt at his feet, hugging Tapiwa's knees and smiling up at him.

Chipo began to warm the soup she had made the day before, a broth with vegetables into which she would break three eggs. She would supplement this with fresh bread she had purchased on her way home.

"My father, I have had such a good day today! Granny and I—"

"She never took him to the clinic!" Chipo snapped. "I told her when to go there and gave her money for antibiotics, and instead, do you know what she did? She—"

"She let me sleep, my father! Then she gave me that awful tea she makes, and some *sadza*, and I played with Coomi, and my ear felt just right!—so we never went to the clinic!" Farai smiled triumphantly at his father. It was acceptable for him to interrupt his mother, though not his father or grandmother.

Tapiwa stroked Farai's left ear, then rubbed harder. Farai smiled again at his own recovery, and then Tapiwa smiled too. "So, by doing this," he said to Chipo, "your mother has repaid us some of the money we give her each month! That is a good thing."

"Well, yes, she did," Chipo grudged. "But he could have

gotten worse. It could have cost us more money and our son more pain. My mother is stubborn. She thinks her old remedies are correct, and she ignores what medical science tells us today. She makes me so angry when she does things like this!"

She stirred the soup hard and splashed some of the precious dinner onto the stove, then spooned the liquid into three chipped bowls and laid them on the table with the round loaf of bread. Three spoons completed the setting. She brought a bowl of water to Tapiwa and Farai and gave them a cloth to wash their hands. Then she sat on one of the stools and gestured to her son and husband to join her.

Tapiwa liked it that Chipo sat with them as they ate. His own mother, now dead, had always served him, his father, and his brothers first, and only after they had satisfied their appetites had she eaten any food that might be left. As for his father's second wife, she had led her life in a separate hut; Tapiwa had seen little of her as he grew up.

Chipo made pretty good company most nights, too, though even when she was in a good mood their dinners tended to be silent; they'd both grown up this way. But tonight she was angry about her mother, and her silence felt heavy.

"I procured our passports today," Tapiwa told her with pride when they had finished and washed their hands again. He would have to wait until Farai went to sleep to share with his wife the terrifying event of the early afternoon. There would be too great a risk of the news getting out if his little son heard what had happened; he might tell his grandmother or his playmates.

"Well, it's about time, with our leaving in two weeks." These were Chipo's only words as she cleaned up after their dinner. Then she took Farai's hand, saying, "Come, now, son, it's time for bed" and they walked out the door to the bathroom. They returned a short time later and she pulled out Farai's pallet and spread it on the floor a few feet away from the bed. Obedient, Farai lay down on it, closed his eyes, and appeared to be asleep.

He was tired after being awake most of the previous night, and she was tired as well.

"Wife, I need to tell you what happened to me this afternoon," Tapiwa whispered as they lay together in the narrow bed. "Are you listening?"

"Please make it short. My day has been full, and I am very tired."

"They kidnapped me, wife! Three men in masks! It was like what has happened with some of our friends!"

Her body jerked rigid against his.

"But you are here. They let you go, then?"

"Well, yes, they did, but first they talked to me about our trip, and they threatened me. They even made foolish threats of monitoring me in California! As if they had the power to do that!" His laugh derided the very idea.

"I am grateful and glad that you are here and safe, and that we will go far away, husband. I have told you many times that your political activities are dangerous, not just to you but to myself and our son. Once again, I beg you not to see those friends who plot to overthrow the government, and not to communicate with them when we are in that faraway place we are going to. And now I truly need to sleep. The day has been full, and the days ahead until we leave will be even more full. Good night, husband." She'd spoken far longer than usual for her, and now she turned her back to him and closed her eyes.

Tapiwa lay quietly on his back for several hours before sleep came, enjoying the warmth of her body and her soft, even breath sounding over the faster breath of his son. He would have liked her to be more sympathetic, but he knew how angry and scared she was. While he and his friends plotted now for liberation, what lurked in *her* mind was her father's early death following his violent removal from her home when she was a child. Tapiwa would have to be content with the way she was for the present.

9

Harare, Zimbabwe
August 1998

Heavy thuds against their locked door splintered the central panel.

Later, Tapiwa couldn't be sure whether Chipo had kicked him in warning before she jumped out of bed or whether the first blow to his body had come from the masked intruders. By the moonlight from the west window, he could see two forms in oversized uniforms, stomping toward him in their knee-high steel-tipped boots.

He was slammed to the floor. He sensed Chipo and Farai cowering beneath the bed out of sight of the intruders. Blows crunched Tapiwa's skull, bashed his groins and the soles of his feet. No one spoke: the only sounds were the thuds of the clubs and, though he tried to keep silent, his own screams and groans. He could smell his fear, and the *Chibuku* on the breath of his attackers. Shameful wetness trickled between his legs.

If only he could control his moans, they might leave him for dead. His lips clamped shut, Tapiwa summoned all his remaining strength and implored the god of his childhood, in whom he had thought he no longer believed. *"Mwari, help me!"* He clamped his upper teeth over his lower lip, willing his body to lie stiff and motionless.

The intruders left as abruptly as they had come. At the broken door, they paused a moment and in unison intoned: *"Mhondoro."*

The family listened together to the sounds of the men's booted feet descending the stairs.

Chipo moved first, crawling from beneath the bed and dragging Farai behind her. "Nothing happened, son. Your father is all right." She laid him back on his pallet and told him, "Close your eyes and go back to sleep, Farai."

Dutiful even at this moment, the boy tried to close his wide eyes. He knew he would be beaten if he disobeyed; that's how things were. Trembling, he turned his back to his parents so his mother could not see his open eyes, and he listened. His father's sobbing had filled him with fear, and there was something different about his mother.

He heard the gentleness. "Here? Does it hurt here?" he heard her ask now.

Tapiwa had fallen silent.

"Don't try to move, husband. I will fetch what is needed."

Farai heard her quick footsteps across the room, the sound of water splashing into the metal pan, and the pan being set gently on the stove. Moments later she returned to Tapiwa, who was still silent as a stone. Farai heard water being wrung from the cloth and could almost feel his mother's gentle rubbing, chafing, probing as if she were tending him, not his father. She muttered under her breath: *"Midzimu,* help us!"

Now he noticed his father's breath too, not regular, but yes! He was breathing. Farai sensed that his mother wouldn't notice if he rolled over again, so he did so, eyes closed, then opened them just a slit.

All his life he would remember what he saw. His father

appeared to be asleep. He watched his mother's tender strokes, saw her lay her wet cheek against his father's and kiss him. "You will be all right, my husband," she crooned, just as his *ambuya* had crooned to him that morning. "I will help you be strong, and we will leave this place and never come back, and we will be together, and we will be happy."

10

Harare International Airport
August 31, 1998

"Cali-for-ni-*yah!*" "Ca-*li*-fornya!" "Cal-i-for—" The word was hard for him to pronounce, but Farai worked earnestly at it.

As in a dream, Tapiwa Moyo, awkward in his new Western suit, stood and regarded his family. The four of them—he and Chipo, Farai, and Ruvimbo—were in the South African Airlines waiting room of the Harare International Airport, a building inspired by the Great Zimbabwe ruins.

In an hour he, Chipo, and Farai would fly from here to Johannesburg, then to Dulles Airport in Washington, DC, and on to Los Angeles. After they left Ruvimbo would return to her cottage with her friend Tatenda, who was waiting outside in a taxi.

Tapiwa looked at Ruvimbo. She was rooted to the floor a few feet from her daughter and grandson. She wore a drab long, full skirt with a shawl; the red and yellow scarf tied tightly around her head leaped out as the only bright note. She maintained her calm, responding absently to Farai as he tried to break through the coolness that separated his mother and grandmother.

"*Ambuya!*" Farai shouted over and over as he ran back and forth between them. "*Amai!*" He wore the short brown pants they had gotten him for the trip and a pair of Western-style sneakers. Ruvimbo had made him the bright green, short-sleeved shirt as a going-away gift.

More than ever, Tapiwa could see the resemblance between his wife and mother-in-law: the same tall, slender frame and the air of strength and dignity. Farai, Tapiwa thought, resembled him more than he did Chipo. Farai was agile and light on his feet, with expressions flitting over his face like sunshine and shadow.

Tapiwa felt an upwelling of love and pride. He tried to look calm and masterful; after all, he was the chief of this family of three people and they depended on him. He fingered the fresh scar on his cheek and with his new slight limp, walked toward them.

If only, he thought. *If only Chipo would unbend a little toward her mother. Put her arm around her.* He knew Ruvimbo's pride would not permit her to make the first move; she stood stiff as a *danda* while Chipo rummaged through her bag for some trifle. The loudspeaker brayed out something unintelligible, and a rumbling metal gate opened, leading toward the ramp to the plane. Chipo took Farai's hand, curtseyed to her mother, then headed toward the gate. Farai broke free and ran to clasp Ruvimbo's knees. "*Chisarai, ambuya, chisarai!*"

Tapiwa watched as Ruvimbo knelt and gave her grandson solemn kisses, first on one cheek, then on the other. "Be well, Farai," she told him, then rose, and offered her son-in-law her right hand, her left hand on her right forearm.

"Go well, my son," she said, then walked away down the corridor toward her waiting taxi. Her step was steady, her head erect.

If only, Tapiwa grieved silently as he followed his wife and son.

If only.

11

Pasadena, California
Wednesday, September 2, 1998

"I hope you like the apartment. As I said, we weren't able to completely finish readying it for you, but you can move in anyway, and the painters should be done a week from now at most."

Alexis Storn, campus liaison for international students, had given them a warm welcome in her office, and was now driving them to their assigned student housing unit. Alexis had sent helpful e-mails to Tapiwa in Harare, and now she confirmed the impression of her they had evoked—competent, pleasant, even sincere. He liked her limberness, her brisk walk, her no-nonsense short haircut, direct glance, and ruddy cheeks. *Perhaps a hiker,* he thought. He had liked the paintings on her office walls as well.

They pulled into a driveway and parked in a lot, then crossed to their new home. Alexis unlocked the apartment door, which creaked open, sagging on its hinges. Farai hung back at first while Tapiwa and Chipo stepped in. The rooms they saw were bare: living room, kitchen, bath, and two small bedrooms. Dust motes danced in the hot sunshine that streamed in. Gray painters' canvasses lay bunched on the floors. The smell of paint bit their throats and noses.

Alexis flicked a switch, lighting a single bulb in the kitchen that was barely visible in the sun's glare. She turned the faucet, and a rusty trickle emerged. "No air conditioning, but the windows are screened, and if you leave them open at night, you shouldn't be too warm. When the colder weather begins, Pasadena Technological Institute—PTI—will issue a space heater for each room. You plug them in, and they burn kerosene. They're fuel efficient, really warm up a room."

They hardly wanted to contemplate warming up a room on this ninety-five-degree afternoon, but Tapiwa and Chipo nodded. "And a bed, table, chairs?" Chipo asked her.

Just then Farai ran in through the open door. Already he had found the tiny children's playground—empty now—not far away and tried out its swing. He'd grasped the metal rail on the stairs to the slide and found it too hot to touch. He'd checked the meager sandbox. He gave his parents a huge smile, his eyes crinkled almost shut.

"*Amai! Baba!* I found a swing outside!"

Tapiwa squatted and held out his arms to his son. "*Mwanakomana*, that is good news indeed." He turned to Alexis. "In Harare we had to walk many blocks from our apartment to the children's park."

Chipo looked at Alexis. "About the furnishings?"

But Alexis delayed her reply for a moment. "How wonderful that your son already speaks some English."

Chipo's and Tapiwa's shoulders straightened as they smiled broadly.

"And did you know that there are other Zimbabweans living in the area? A small group in Los Angeles, I've been told—it's only twenty minutes away. And I think I've also heard that a Zimbabwean woman is on the child care staff over at the Pasadena Child Development Center—we call it PCDC. It almost could be called the International Children's Center, there are so many staff and children from around the world! I'll take you and Farai to visit tomorrow, Chipo, and we'll ask Hannah about that—Hannah's the PCDC director.

"But you asked about furnishings. Yes, today's a Wednesday and"—she looked at her watch—"the second-hand furniture loan on campus will still be open. It's run by volunteer faculty wives. They should be able to lend you all you need. Would you like me to take you now? We can use my van to bring back the essentials." Chipo's eyes filled at this kindness. Not trusting her voice, she only nodded.

Alexis locked the door behind them, then drove them down tree-shaded streets to what looked like an old garage on campus, tucked away behind the physical plant building. She took them down a flight of stairs to a cavernous basement stacked with every sort of furniture as well as kitchen tools, presided over by two gentle-looking older women. Chipo bent her knees and Tapiwa bowed as Alexis presented them.

The ladies introduced the family to a young woman named Sue Bowles, who was about to leave with a basket of cutlery, plates, and glasses. *She looks as if she's come here straight from her bed*, Tapiwa thought. Her red hair lay stringy and tousled and there were imprints from a pillow on her left cheek. Her clothing looked stained and wrinkled, her shoulders sagged, and her steps dragged, but she gave them a warm smile.

"This furniture loan's great! Alan and I got outfitted here when we arrived last year, and I'm back now for a few more things. Don't know what we'd do without these ladies." She gestured toward the two older women, one of whom was pushing a baby carriage toward the back of the room. A high chair and portable baby seat also stood near the ladies' desk, as if these things had just been returned.

"I have a son, Aaron, four years old. He's staying with a friend this afternoon. How old's your son?" Sue asked them, glancing toward Farai. The three parents brightened as they exchanged child-the-same-age pleasantries.

Later, back in their new dwelling, Alexis helped them unload the items they had borrowed, talking all the while about the Pasadena Child Development Center. "The center operates in six old houses scattered here and there over several blocks on the edge of campus. Farai will be happy there, I can assure you," she told his parents. "It'll make his transition from Zimbabwe to Southern California so much easier. He'll make friends and learn a lot too. The center teachers really understand young children." She set down two empty drawers in the bedroom as Tapiwa and Chipo brought in a low dresser. Farai carried in pillows for a sofa.

"I hear happy things all the time from students and faculty with children at the center! It's so fortunate that Tapiwa's fellowship includes PCDC tuition—many international students' fellowships do not."

Alexis arranged a time for Chipo to visit the child care center in the morning, then left them to arrange their things.

Tapiwa told his wife, "I felt something sad about that woman, Sue, whom we met today, the one with the son. She talked with us, but her eyes were far away, did you not think?"

But Chipo was preoccupied. "This house is bigger than our apartment, and I won't have to climb stairs each day, but it's a little lonely. I wonder where our neighbors are."

"Classes don't begin until next week. I believe that what is called Labor Day is coming up, Chipo. People often go on holiday before that day."

They laid mattresses on the floors of both bedrooms, and Chipo set the kitchen table for their first dinner in the home where they planned to spend the next two years. Then she and Tapiwa and Farai went out to explore their neighborhood. Alexis had directed them to a Superette only five blocks away. They experienced the strangeness of this market where, without bartering and under one roof, one could buy bread, milk, ground meat, and vegetables. Returning home, Chipo and Tapiwa walked quickly while their son capered ahead of them, craning his neck at every car, house, and person he passed. He waited dutifully for his parents at each corner, crossing the streets with them.

"Husband, it is well that we are here. I am glad."

Tapiwa straightened his shoulders in pleasure for the second time today, this time responding to his wife's warmth. He took her hand and squeezed it.

"And I am glad also."

12

The next morning Chipo followed Alexis' directions and rode the city bus with her son to the corner of Hill and Del Monte, just a few blocks from the PCDC building. As Alexis had told her, it housed Hannah's upstairs office, two "fours" groups, and a "threes" group. The building looked like a former modest family home, wooden with old-fashioned French windows that opened outward on this mild morning, and gables jutting over the second story. Painted yellow, it needed repainting. Massive piles of pine needles lay on the slanted roof, deposits from two tall trees that shaded the yard. Chipo saw several children: a boy painted at an easel, two girls climbed on a wooden play structure, and a boy and a girl swung high and swooped low on a swing. A teacher and a boy chanted and twirled a jump rope that sang through the air, while a girl navigated it with steady rhythm.

> Pease porridge *hot!*
> Pease porridge *cold !*
> Pease porridge *in* the pot,
> Nine days *old!*

Alexis waited for Chipo near the redwood fence surrounding the yard, then guided her into one of the classrooms. Here Chipo noted bold, bright paintings on the walls and small, open cubbies, each labeled with a child's name and holding his or her possessions. Child-sized chairs surrounded low tables laid out with wooden puzzles, scissors, crayons, and old magazines. On the floor in a corner stood an intricate structure made of blocks; two girls and a boy lay on their stomachs as they added to it, chattering and moving tiny cars and people up and down what they had created. On open shelves behind them, Chipo saw bins of LEGO sets, puzzles, and rows and rows of brightly colored books.

Farai walked in a small circle in the middle in the classroom, absorbing the activities around him, ready to join in immediately and oblivious of his mother.

"I think he's ready, all right," Alexis told Chipo, indicating the stairs to Hannah's office. The narrow treads creaked and the two women turned sideways to let a young woman, also turned sideways, pass them. Farai squeezed forward through the remaining thread of space. At the top of the stairs they made a sharp U-turn to the left, moved down a short, dark hall, and emerged in a tiny room containing two desks with computers on them, an ancient refrigerator, a copy machine, and a printer on a small table. On the wall Chipo noted a quotation by Jean Piaget. She remembered him from her studies at the University of Harare. Had it been a lecture about the history of scientific thought?

> *Knowledge cannot be "given" to children. To learn, children must discover and construct through activities.*

13

Hannah sat facing them, her back to the oak branches swaying outside the lone window at the back of the room. Then she was on her feet, moving toward the boy and his mother. "You must be Farai; I'm so glad to see you," she said, and "Welcome to California, Chipo; I'm Hannah." She gave Farai a basket of LEGO bricks and a small train set, pointing to a corner for him to play, then asked Chipo about the trip from Zimbabwe.

"You're in good hands, Chipo," Alexis interrupted briefly, "and I'll be getting back to my office now. Be sure to call with any questions or needs." With that, she disappeared down the hall.

Chipo sat stiffly on the chair Hannah indicated. Hannah pulled her own chair around the desk and seated herself next to her, presenting her with a folder marked *Moyo*. Inside were enrollment forms and a parent handbook. Hannah walked Chipo through center procedures and answered her questions. Gradually the younger woman began to relax, even smiling once or twice.

The three returned downstairs and out to a play yard, where Hannah introduced Chipo and Farai to Joan Nefas. Farai watched the activities in the yard for a moment, then edged over to an easel where clean white paper awaited him. He dipped a long, fat brush into brilliant paint and in one swift motion created a luscious scarlet mandala, then turned to see its effect on his mother, who made no response.

"It's a good sign that he would plunge right in like that," Hannah told Chipo. Then to Farai she said, "Your painting looks alive and breathing, Farai! After it's dried, maybe you'll want to take it home to show your dad." Farai nodded and resumed his brushwork.

"I've never seen a play yard like this for children," Chipo told Hannah. "We have parks at home, but most children do not go to school until they are five or six, or even seven. How long may he stay here today, please?"

They agreed that she would return in three hours, and Chipo started toward the exit gate.

"Let him know you're leaving, please, and that you'll be back soon," Hannah instructed, and Chipo turned back and followed her suggestion. Farai nodded, continuing his painting while Chipo and Hannah went back inside. Then Hannah remembered something.

"An African woman named Sekai Torino works on our staff, in the infant room. The infant building's three blocks away. Perhaps one day you'd like me to walk you over there so you could talk with her?"

"Sekai is an African name, all right. In fact my mother's dearest friend had that name. Turino, that is not African. But yes, Hannah, thank you, I should very much like to do that one day. I will let you know when I am more settled, all right?" Chipo gave Hannah one of her rare smiles. "Until two o'clock, then?"

Watching Chipo walk gracefully toward the exit, Hannah mused about what a balanced, healthy boy Farai appeared to be. Not all children found it as easy to enter into the life of the center on their first day. This was a happy beginning, to be sure.

She looked forward to meeting his father as well. She wondered, though: wasn't Chipo a little frozen, somehow? Had she no apprehensions about leaving her son alone with strangers on what was only their second day in California?

14

She stood out among the few women in the lab. Tapiwa noticed Elaine early on, when classes at PTI began at the end of September: tanned, with streaked brown hair, luscious skin, warm blue eyes, full lips set in what seemed like a perpetual smile, and an invitational gaze. Dressed scantily in the warm weather, her heaviness slowed her down a little, but her wide hips swayed delightfully when she moved and her cleavage accentuated full breasts, causing Tapiwa to forget that he had thought he preferred slenderness.

He'd always enjoyed women, and at home they'd flocked to him, but he'd been content with Chipo's passion when they were alone and her traditional deference in public—though sometimes she did speak first, or say edgy things, or just "walk mad" when she disagreed with him. So far, Tapiwa hadn't strayed. His own father had had two wives, but Tapiwa—though he enjoyed toying with the idea now and then—felt one was ample.

He felt proud and happy to be in Pasadena, to know that his good grades at the University of Zimbabwe had brought him here. None of his fellow Pasadena students knew this, of course;

to them, he was just one of the rare black students, with a weird British accent. If any of his professors had bothered to look at his records, they gave no sign of being impressed. In the classroom lectures, they droned on, pausing now and then to write endless dense formulas on the blackboard. Tapiwa grasped most of the diagrammed information, but the American English sounded like gibberish to him at first. He tried to strike up conversations with some of the male students, but they seemed stressed, burdened with the heavy classroom assignments. He felt little reciprocity.

He was lonely, and on top of that, he shared the common anxiety about failing. Everyone knew that at the end of each semester, some students did not return. One man had hanged himself in his dormitory room the previous spring. The administration had redoubled its efforts to ease the campus ambiance, but it was an uphill struggle: everyone knew PTI to be "a cut above"; it admitted only brilliant students and most of its faculty were internationally known and honored. Professors' schedules were full of research trips, committee meetings, publication dates, and—with help from graduate students like Tapiwa—gathered data for their projects.

"Where're you from?" Elaine had asked him the first day in the lab. "I'm thinking maybe Africa, with that accent you have?" She gave him a warm smile. "I'm Elaine," she added, "Elaine Sark."

"Yes, Miss. I'm from Zimbabwe." He saw her blank expression and added, "It is in East Africa. In the middle. No ocean."

"No ocean? You mean landlocked? How does your country trade, then?"

He saw that she listened carefully and that she thought about what she heard. "We depend on trains and trucks to get our goods to boats," he told her. "They go through Mozambique, to the east of us, when things aren't too upset there."

"Oh." She seemed to have no further curiosity about Zimbabwe. "Are you here alone?"

"No, my wife and little son are here with me. We're getting settled up there"—he gestured north toward the hills above Pasadena— "in the married student housing."

She made a face. "Pretty grim, isn't it?" A pause. "Well, if you ever have trouble with our assignments, come over to my place. I live right across the street from the campus, on DeWitt Street next door to the park. I could probably help."

So bold! The very first time they had spoken! Tapiwa felt a mixture of surprise and pleasure. It seemed obvious that she found him attractive. He would have to think about it.

15

UCLA ECE 240; Developmental EC Administration
Assignment: observe and describe an indoor or outdoor setting at your center. Write everything you see and also include background information when needed, as well as brief descriptions, associations, and thoughts you may have about what you observe. Do not exceed five pages.

Time and date: 10 a.m., Thursday, 1/14/99
Location: One of two play yards for fours, at PCDC.
Description (brief): A mild, sunny morning. Twenty children, lead teacher Anne Williams, and three other staff, including William Brost, mentioned below, a total of twenty-five human beings in this yard.
Observer: Hannah Cooper
Number of pages: 5

Chipo Moyo's arrival with her four-year-old son Farai is the first thing I see when I arrive to observe Anne's fours yard. The center opens at six thirty, and it's unusual for parents and their kids to arrive after nine in the morning. Farai and his family have only recently come here from Zimbabwe. He dashes into the yard ahead of his mother, who's scowling. "Farai, come and tell me good-bye properly!" she commands in that peremptory British accent of hers, but when he approaches she gives him only a perfunctory kiss on his forehead, turns her back to him, goes next door to Joan's yard to sign him in, and leaves with no further word to anyone.

Sue Bowles, another center parent, arrives moments later, holding her four-year-old son Aaron's hand. As usual, she looks lonely and her eyes are lifeless, but she summons her energy, kneels to Aaron's level, puts both arms around him, and holds him a moment. "I love you, son," she tells him before releasing him to run to his new buddy, Farai. Farai and Aaron often visit Anne's yard. They're in Joan's group, but only Anne offers the carpentry projects that both boys love.

Anne, the lead teacher in this group of fours, helps Aaron, Farai, and a little girl adjust C-clamps to the table and select wood scraps from a box at their feet. In her late twenties, Anne's tall, slender, and rather plain, with straight brown hair parted in the center and tucked behind her ears. She never effuses and rarely laughs. Sometimes her straight-out, "tell it like it is" manner distances parents, but not children, who feel her warmth and know they can trust her.

She pulls a small camera from her pocket and photographs Farai Moyo as he hammers his "boat"—two pieces of wood that he'll paint next week, then sail under a bridge on the stream that flows through one part of the PTI campus. Farai and Aaron made this plan a week ago with Anne and two or three other children. When their project's finished, Anne will write it up on a poster, illustrated with photos of the process—from the original brainstorming session to hammering, nailing, painting, and then walking on campus to the stream and sailing the boats. The poster will go on the wall where all can see and enjoy it.

Suddenly, as happens for me from time to time, a golden,

shimmering light enfolds the whole scene before me, weaving through and around the many interacting people and activities. It's a moment of grateful perception of the miracle I'm observing—the miracle of a happy, purposeful group of children and adults working together.

In a few seconds it splinters into fragments: Su-Ling skins her knee and needs comforting; Celia and Tim appear to be on the verge of blows over a scooter. I become aware of Sue Bowles' hungry and odd, possessive gaze at Farai and her son Aaron.

Rocky best describes Sue's life in recent months. She and her husband Alan lost their three-month-old daughter Sophie to pneumonia almost on the eve of his long-planned research trip to South America this fall. Sue and Alan talked it over and decided he should make the trip anyway, as the grant has a fixed deadline that can't be extended. He'll be away for several months, leaving Sue free, in theory, to pursue her own PhD dissertation. Not surprisingly, however, she finds it impossible to concentrate on research and writing; instead she seems ever more focused on Aaron, with a maternal attraction to his friend Farai.

"He and Aaron get along so well," she told me a few days ago. "When Farai comes to our place it's almost like having a baby sitter—they never argue or get into trouble. It's like they're on the same brain wave. Would you believe, last Saturday afternoon they spent *six hours* building a city with Aaron's blocks? I had to drag them away to get them to eat peanut butter sandwiches!"

Then she confided, "With things so messed up at Chipo's, I'm thinking of asking her if maybe Farai could move in with us for awhile."

"Sue, I imagine Chipo's fairly lonely right now—" I started to say that day, but she cut me off.

"Don't talk to me about her! I hear her with Farai—she's mean to him a lot. Tells him his dad's no good, yanks him along by the wrist when they get off the bus. I don't mean to be uncharitable, Hannah, but it's Farai's good I'm considering! Right now she's not in any condition to give him what he needs."

I knew Sue's own mental state to be shaky. I didn't know what to say to her that day, rationalizing my silence with the knowledge that she sees a therapist every week. Her eyes weren't focused, and it almost seemed she wanted to own her son's friendship and replace Chipo as Farai's mother. *If she could only befriend Chipo,* I thought to myself, *these two lone mothers could find a lot in common.*

I make a mental note to talk with Sue again soon. It's lunchtime, and the gentle beat and jingle of William's tambourine calls the children inside to wash their hands.

We do offer staff this one decent benefit, the hot lunch, I think, and I focus on the happy sight of the group taking their meal together. Some days I join them; more often I take lunch at my desk as I work.

Today I have time to enjoy my sack lunch with them, and I'm happy to lose myself in their company. Aaron comes over to me. "Hannah, how come you've been sitting and writing in our yard this morning?" he asks.

"I'm still going to school, and my teacher gives me jobs to do," I explain. "One of them is writing down what I see at our center, like you do here sometimes, Aaron, with Anne helping you."

"When you do it, you look like it's hard work, Hannah, not fun like when Anne helps me write. How come?" Curiosity raised his eyebrows.

"I'm not sure, my friend. Maybe it's because I really want the words to be right and say what I truly see."

"That should be easy," he told me gravely, patting my hand. "Maybe I can help you next time you do it."

16

Harare
October 15, 1998

My Dear Sekai,

I was truly glad to have your letter in September, and your news that by working four days a week you can manage to stretch Steve's pension far enough to stay in your Pasadena apartment for now. And you say you have a car! Even though it's an old one, here at home you'd be considered wealthy, believe me! You didn't say what your job is, only that you like it and it doesn't pay much, but will help you get work credits toward Social Security later. You and Steve were wise to aim for your U.S. citizenship when you first went there. I know you miss home, but it's good you'll have Social Security and Medicare when you get to sixty-five years—hey, that's only sixteen years away for us, do you believe it?!

To me it sounds as if you've made wise decisions and are doing well, and I certainly understand your plan to remain there.

I have an Internet café near where I live. Mugabe finally permitted e-mail here, just last year—he worries a *lot* about outside communication. I wonder if you have e-mail access too, maybe at your job. It would be fun to write you that way, because actual letters in and out of our country do often disappear, or take months to get delivered. Of course censorship of the e-mail has to be taken into account, which could be a disadvantage.

Well, Chipo did send me a card from Pasadena, telling me where she's living. She and Tapiwa are settled in, in a student housing unit on North Roosevelt Avenue. Is that anywhere near you? If you should go by one day, maybe you could give me a description of the place. You can imagine how I miss Farai, my only grandchild—I saw him rarely here in Harare, mostly only when he fell sick and Chipo couldn't find anyone else to stay with him, but at least I felt him close by.

Stay well, dear friend.

Ruvimbo

17

November 1998

"What are you afraid of, Tapiwa—oh, did I say your name right?" Elaine had caught up with him as he left the lab building.

How could she be so forward? He quickened his step and kept his eyes facing front, though he had already seen that she wore pink sandals with heels and a brown miniskirt with a short-sleeved fuzzy pink sweater. She dressed up more than the other women students; he'd noticed that too.

"Come on, Tapiwa, I won't bite, honest! Did you get that probability question? I think maybe it's a trick. Sometimes the profs like to give us trick questions, just to keep us on our toes." She laughed and stood on her toes for a moment.

She enchanted him, no doubt about it. "It is difficult for me, but I think I will be able to get it." He looked away from her.

"Well, any time you have trouble, you're always welcome at my place. I live just over there," she said, pointing toward the dorm for single grad students. "Actually, I'm the only woman living there," she drawled. "You might want to see how single grads live, Tapiwa. Unless you're *afraid*, of course."

"I—"

"It's okay, Tapiwa, I understand." She chuckled, deep and low. "Catch you another time!"

He turned, saw her hurrying off in the direction she'd indicated. His heart thumped, his face felt hot. What did he feel? This was 1998, he reminded himself. Even at home no one any longer took two wives. In the seventies, having two wives as his father did had already been a dying arrangement in their village. Men might enjoy other women but no longer provided huts and support for more than one.

When he and Chipo had married six years earlier, she'd been very clear about what she expected of him—what did she call it?—"twentieth-century commitment," that was it. She would not be his servant, she'd said. Whatever she brought to their marriage would be brought from her love, not from duty, and she expected him to do his part to keep their love fresh. It was hard to do that sometimes, with Chipo so moody, withdrawing now and then into herself for no reason he could see.

Why was this girl Elaine suddenly making it so difficult for him? She was dangerous—he could see that—pretending to question his manhood so as to lure him into her life. What did she want from him? And how would it be to go with her to her apartment, put his hands on those two incredible breasts, kiss her so deep and hard she would open her legs and thrust her pelvis to his. He would press his to hers, until—but where were his thoughts racing? He would go home *now*, home to Chipo and their son. He pictured Farai rubbing his ears and laughing, singing himself to sleep, wriggling out of his bed in the morning, swinging outside alone. Tapiwa's step became more resolute, and as he strode, he smiled to himself.

18

November 1998

Late that afternoon, Tapiwa's bus climbed the hill above Pasadena Technological Institute to the student housing project on Roosevelt Avenue. He had heard how these former army barracks had been constructed in what used to be an unincorporated area just north of Pasadena. Shortly after World War II it had become clear that graduate students, many of them veterans, tended to be in their mid-twenties or older and to have wives and children, and PTI had reluctantly transported and placed the barracks here at that time. This was done nearly thirty years before PTI admitted women as students, and accommodations for them were seen as a distraction and an inconvenience.

All in all, Tapiwa mused, his living unit felt slightly more spacious and comfortable than their former Harare apartment, but neither seemed built to nurture its residents.

On his way in he saw Farai swinging forlornly in the children's play area not far from their back door, where Chipo could keep an eye on him through the kitchen window.

"Hello, my wife," Tapiwa greeted her.

Chipo didn't answer right away, and he could read her feelings from her quick, loud step as she laid dinner on their table.

"Greetings, husband," she answered sullenly as she continued to carry food and plates to the table.

"Something's wrong, isn't it?" he asked, seating himself in the single armchair in their living-dining area. "Tell me, wife, what is it?"

Chipo wasn't accustomed to sharing her concerns with Tapiwa, but she had no one else to tell them to. "I miss my job, I guess," she told him. "All I do here is take Farai to the child care, go to the market, come home and cook, go back to the child care for Farai, and come home again. It's boring."

She stopped laying out the dinner, walked over to Tapiwa, and sat down across from him.

He spoke sharply. "Farai gets so much from the center, and we're so fortunate that the fellowship pays for it. Can't you think of your son and not yourself?"

"Oh, I'm grateful for his sake—I really am. But I have needs, too, you know. What about me, husband, *what about me*?" A lone tear dripped off Chipo's chin, and she wiped her nose on her sleeve.

"Well, maybe I could stop at the child care and get Farai sometimes," Tapiwa told her. This was a new thought for him, but he'd seen other fathers leave the center with their children. It was on his way to the bus stop from his lab; he could do this once in a while, he supposed. Why not?

Chipo held on to her dissatisfaction. "I guess that would help a little," she told Tapiwa, "but I still don't know what to do with my days. If only I could work here! Why can't you get me a work permit? We could use the money."

Tapiwa's face darkened. "You wish we had more money?"

"It's not so much the money, it's just that I'm used to working. And I miss my friends at home too, even though I don't look forward to returning to the dangers there." She glanced out the window at Farai sitting motionless on the swing.

"We knew it would be difficult when we decided to come," he reminded her. "And our being here will make things so much better when we go back. Can't you keep that in your mind?" Out of nowhere, Elaine's inviting glance and manner suddenly filled his mind.

Chipo sighed as she felt his disengagement from their conversation. They'd spoken these words before and they seemed to go nowhere. They had a room of their own now, with Farai in his own bedroom next to theirs, but she knew she'd be cold to Tapiwa tonight. She felt imprisoned in her coldness.

"I'm sorry, husband," she told him. "I just feel so sad, and I can't seem to forget it. I don't want to bring you sadness, but that is how I feel."

❧   ❧   ❧

The next week, on a Saturday morning, Farai came in from the play area and looked at his father and mother. "Father," he blurted, "will you take me to Elaine's again soon? The swings in the park by her place are better than the ones here."

Tapiwa instantly looked toward Chipo. Her expression was impassive. He attempted to replicate her calm demeanor, his body still, eyes half shut.

Only a fool would have taken Farai to Elaine's.
What was Chipo thinking?

19

December 1998

Heavy, was how Sue Bowles felt. Heavy limbs. Heavy heart. Heavy stomach. Heavy brain. Maybe today she could just lie here in the big empty bed. Aaron could get his own breakfast, and go to PCDC by himself.

Right. Sure. A four-year-old can do all that. Would he drive their funky Dodge Dart to the center or take the bus, then cross busy Del Monte Boulevard by himself and walk the several blocks to his building at PCDC?

"Mom," Aaron called from the next room, "I'm almost ready. When're we leaving?"

He loved the center; Sue felt glad of that. He especially loved his friend Farai, and at least two of his teachers, Anne and William. She never had to force him out of bed, then force his clothes on him, shirt then socks then pants then shoes, the way it would have been if he didn't like the center so much.

But *she* was a different story. She dragged one leg out of bed, then the other. Panties, bra, slacks, tee, socks on this cold morning and Birkenstocks, oh God what an effort. Without

Aaron's presence and needs, she would never dress, never eat, never do another thing in her life. She'd just lie in the bed, doze and dream, get up now and then to pee, and even that would demand a teeth-clenching summoning of energy.

I may be twenty-seven, but I feel like an infant. Maybe it's my way of grieving Sophie. Did Phyllis tell me something like that at our last session?

Then she came back to reality, back to Aaron. Maybe a bagel for his breakfast. He'd have a hot lunch at the center, thankfully. Sue stirred and stretched on the bed.

She heard Aaron's voice again: "Mom, remember you asked William for dinner? I think it's tonight."

20

Aaron hadn't brought it up since his mother, in a burst of spontaneity, had surprised him one afternoon last week in the play yard when she'd asked his teacher to their home. Aaron had learned that sometimes she said things she didn't mean, forgot things she'd arranged.

Dad had talked with him about this in their parked car outside their house after he'd picked up Aaron from the center; it was on the day before he left for South America. Dad had asked him to climb over into the front seat next to him, had put his arm around him. Dad's arm felt so good, holding him close.

"I'll be back soon, son," he'd said. "Mom and I decided I should do this trip. I'll be working hard and I'll think of you the whole time. Mom's pretty shaky since Sophie left us, but she's stronger every day. I know you can help her and be there for her. I count on you, Aaron."

Aaron had thrown both arms around his father and solemnly assured him that he could do what he asked.

21

In the early winter dusk Aaron skipped ahead of his teacher, William Brost, up the walk to the backyard bungalow where he lived with his mother, and threw open the door. William parked his motorcycle and caught up with him there. No aroma of the spaghetti dinner Sue had promised streamed out to welcome them; instead, stale air spiraled slowly through their senses. Aaron switched on a lamp next to the sagging sofa. In the silence they could see a crusted breakfast plate on the table, thick layers of ants oscillating over it. Looking around the room, William saw closed, dusty windows with blinds but no curtains. A faded rug covered the worn, wide, painted floorboards. Besides the table, three upright chairs, and the sofa, he saw no other furniture except shelves filled with Aaron's blocks, and a desk nearby. On it were a closed laptop, scrawled notes, literary journals, and stacks of books. The books, William knew, were mostly by and about the poet Emily Dickinson.

Sue's dissertation, William also knew from Sue's brief confidences in the fours play yard, had ground to a standstill. Her thesis advisor/ professor taught across the country at Boston

University, where Sue had been a graduate student before she married Alan and accompanied him to PTI a year ago. Less and less often, she still tried to work on her dissertation, in touch with her advisor by e-mail and phone. Usually reticent, Sue occasionally shared bits of information about herself with William at the center. It seemed she trusted him because Aaron did.

Where was she? William and Aaron removed their helmets, and Aaron went into his mother's bedroom where she sat on the edge of the rumpled bed rubbing her eyes. She was fully dressed from the morning drive to PCDC with Aaron; even the Birkenstocks were still on her feet.

"I'm sorry, honey," she croaked. "What time is it? I just lay down for a little morning nap—you know I couldn't sleep again last night, Aaron."

He nodded, silent.

Sue turned to William, who stood hesitant now in the bedroom doorway.

"Hello, William. I'm so sorry. Sometimes I have to set two alarm clocks to wake myself up."

"Oh Mom," Aaron quavered, "you didn't remember about William?"

"It's okay, Sue," William cut in. "I know it's a hard time for you right now. How about Aaron and I do the dinner?"

"Shit!" Sue wailed, "I don't even have the stuff in the house. Well, maybe some pasta. But no sauce, no parmesan, no salad makings. I meant to get them on the way home this morning, but I clean forgot."

"It's fine," said William. "Aaron and I, we're good cooks, aren't we, buddy? We'll just whip out to Eddie's Grocery and get us a few things. You put on the pot for pasta, Sue—we'll be right back."

Sue's features and even her body were suddenly energized. "I accept, kind sir, and bring a bottle of something red—you're over twenty-one, aren't you?" Sparked by William's kindness, she rose with more ease than usual. She smoothed the wrinkled sheets and covers, plumped the pillows.

"Okay, my lady." William, wanting to appear cool, tried not to show his disorientation at her sudden change of mood. "We're on our way!"

Aaron and his teacher re-donned their helmets and left, and Sue went to the small kitchen-dining-living room and began to clear the breakfast things. She sprayed and wiped the table and rinsed the dishes. Then she put the pasta water to boil and straightened the kitchen counter. Opposite the front door were built-in drawers and a mirror, part of the charm of this old bungalow. She rummaged for candles and candle holders in the top drawer, found two of each, and placed them on the table. Then she entered Aaron's tiny bedroom on the other side of the main room from her own and pulled up the covers on his bed.

She walked out to the garden. The backyard of a larger home that faced the street, it shielded her bungalow from traffic and passersby. Planted seventy years ago, this garden had been landscaped to last. Eight-foot oleander shrubs grew along the sides, and in the center towered a tulip tree, with clumps of birds-of-paradise at its base—orange and blue splendor year round. Low clusters of white alyssum breathed out their honey fragrance. She and Alan had trimmed and pruned last summer, before Sophie's illness and death, and the little garden looked tidy, colorful, and welcoming. She and Alan had planned to remove the oleanders in the spring, when Sophie would have been old enough to possibly ingest one of its poisonous leaves or blooms. Aaron, almost five, understood about oleanders, poinsettias, and poison oak.

I love this little green world. I feel almost safe here.

How her thoughts wandered. She clipped a few white oleander blossoms and a bird-of-paradise. Back inside she put water and the flowers into in an empty mayonnaise jar and set it on the table, along with three plates and three forks.

"What am I doing?" she mused aloud. "You'd think I was getting ready for Alan." She shook her head but continued to straighten the room, then went to the bathroom, where she combed her hair and applied lipstick. "I haven't done this any time lately," she said aloud and shook her head again.

The roar of William's motorcycle died to a purr as tires scrunched on gravel. She looked out to see Aaron and William as they crossed the yard toward the bungalow. Aaron smiled and talked fast as he danced around William—like a puppy, she thought. As for William, he looked like a natural older brother to Aaron. Both had large heads, thick shocks of brown hair, bright eyes. Their cheeks were ruddy, their lips full. They had similar builds too, if you allowed for the seventeen-year age difference: broad shoulders, well-developed torso, a little short in the leg. The Irish look. The look of her own uncles and grandfather.

Six degrees of difference between any two humans, isn't that all they say there are? These two could certainly be taken for cousins or brothers. She opened the door and called out a welcome to them.

"Mom, you look great!" Aaron shouted.

William gave her an admiring look. "Is the water boiling? Sit down, Sue—we'll fix dinner. You deserve to be spoiled a little."

"Let me put on some music," she said, and when William nodded she chose a favorite Sam Hinton disk of Aaron's. Mellow guitar chords warmed the room, and the endearing words of "Whoever Shall Have Some Good Peanuts" set them humming. Sue sat and watched her son eagerly carrying out the simple tasks William assigned him: he put the salad greens into a bowl, found some dressing, opened the jars of spaghetti sauce they'd bought at the store, grated the lump of parmesan cheese. Aaron kept up a steady stream of questions, almost ignoring his mother.

He's used to cooking projects at the center with William,

Sue thought, and felt warmth seep through her body for the first time in months. William brought her a glass of Merlot. She took a sip, then gasped. "Oh—I almost forgot, I can't have alcohol with the meds I take right now."

I wouldn't share such personal information with anyone at the center except Hannah or Anne, she mused, and shook her head again. What's happening here? Not to worry, she assured herself; William's just a boy—in his early twenties at most.

"Dinner's ready!" William announced with a flourish, and they sat down to eat. They talked at first about the carpentry project Aaron was working on with Farai. William went on to say, "Too bad about Chipo and Tapiwa, isn't it?" but he and Sue both knew they couldn't discuss this in Aaron's presence, and the conversation veered to William's biology studies at nearby Cal State Los Angeles, then to Alan's e-mails home, sent from his research ship off the shores of Colombia. William asked Sue how her own work was coming along.

"Not well, William," she said. "I just can't seem to get myself to go ahead with it. It doesn't help any that my advisor's back in Massachusetts, where I can't see her. She lets me call her at home, though. I talk with her now and then when it's four p.m. here and seven there. She knows about Sophie, and about Alan being away right now, and she understands.

"I have my days free while Aaron's at the center, but—" her voice trailed off.

They had eaten their fill, and now they both looked at Aaron. His eyelids were drooping. Sue excused herself to run Aaron's bath, and supervised as he brushed his teeth.

"Mom, you haven't checked my teeth in ages!" Aaron's words were a protest, but his wide eyes and smile were happy. He did as she asked, then let her bathe him. He pulled on one of his father's clean T-shirts. "Maybe you'll read to me tonight too?" He gave her a hopeful glance.

"Son, I'm sorry about all those other nights," Sue told him.

"Go ahead and pick out a book." He chose a science book with illustrations of turtles.

From the doorway of Aaron's bedroom she told William, "I'm going to read to Aaron for a while. Don't feel you should stay. I'll see you in the morning. Thanks for everything."

She sat at the edge of Aaron's bed and held the book so he could see the pictures. They discussed the differences in tortoise appearance and habits. Sue could hear the clatter of dishes in the next room. Aaron, comfortably relaxed on his pillow, gradually dozed and fell deeply asleep.

His bedside clock said eight thirty. She turned off the lamp and closed his door almost all the way so that only a little light could enter from the other room. Then she tiptoed out and found William washing the last of their dinner dishes. He'd also done the few from breakfast.

"Where do you live, William?" she asked, wondering for the first time. "Somewhere near Cal State?" Embarrassment kept her from thanking him for the cleanup.

"Yeah, I have a room in a home there, in a mostly Mexican neighborhood. Nice family."

"You speak Spanish then?"

"Doesn't everyone who grew up in Southern California, at least a little? My best buddy in grade school was Mexican-American. His folks were very protective, wouldn't let him visit our place, but they always welcomed me in theirs. It felt like my second home, and his mom was my second mom. Sometimes my own mom didn't seem to understand as well as Maria did ..." His voice shook suddenly, and tears thickened his voice.

"Oh William, is she ..."

"Yes, this last summer. Cancer." He sat down at the table where they'd just shared chatter and laughter, dropped his arms and head on it, and sobbed.

Sue pulled another chair close and laid her arm tightly around his shoulders, then tugged her chair with her other hand and sat so they nearly faced each other. Her knees held one of his between them as she embraced him and pulled his head to her chest. His sobs shuddered and racked both their bodies. She stroked his back steadily. Gradually he quieted, raised his head, and looked at her. They stood and walked to Sue's bedroom.

At least when she tried to remember it later, she supposed they must have walked there. After his look and their sudden rising together, she only remembered their struggle in bed to undress each other while devouring each others' mouths. They hadn't wanted to stop kissing even for a second, wrestling with bra hooks and zippers and the whole problem of removing their legs from pants, and the frustration of having to pull their pants up again so shoes could be loosened and shaken off.

With Alan, Sue might have laughed at these setbacks and hindrances, but this was different. Her sudden need for William, and his for her, overwhelmed all.

His thrusting inside her felt like brilliant noonday sun in a place too long dark and cold. In seconds they reached a point of unbearable heat, when consciousness slips away and at the same time heightens. Joyously they gave to each other and joyfully they received. Then they lay together for a few moments, she above him. She shuddered and climaxed again. Quiet now, he looked at her with wonderment.

She wriggled away and struggled into her robe with as much urgency as when she'd undressed a few moments earlier. She hugged it to her and tiptoed quickly from her room to Aaron's. Relief throbbed through her when she saw him still asleep, his thick brown hair falling over his forehead and his hand on the book they'd been reading. She heard his steady breath, noted the slight flush on his cheeks. The clock by his bedside registered only nine ten. How could that be? She sped back to William and lay down beside him without removing her robe. For the first time since Sophie's death, she felt a natural, enveloping drowsiness, altogether different from her drugged sleep earlier that day. Her eyes closed, and she tumbled into deep slumber.

22

December 1998

Elaine's phone ringer was turned to low so that only a scratchy hum wakened her at two o'clock that dark morning.

"Tapiwa," growled a male voice, and she handed him the receiver across the bed.

Who besides Chipo, Tapiwa wondered, knew he could be reached here? And even though Chipo knew, he had forbidden her to call him here. His heart thumped, hurting his chest, his throat. Were Chipo and Farai safe?

"*Mhoro,*" he spoke into the receiver, and waited.

Silence. Then a hoarse, guttural voice barked at him in Shona: "We know you're not with Chipo, Tapiwa. Why are you with the American woman? Remember your agreement. You must return home in twenty months. If you don't, you won't live to regret it, nor will your wife, your son, or your wife's mother. We know *everything*, Tapiwa. You are always in our sight."

A long pause. A single word: "*Mhondoro.*" A loud, abrupt click.

Silence.

23

Pasadena
December 10, 1998

Dear Ruvimbo,

So good to have your letters from home. Since my parents' deaths, I get very little mail from there. I don't have e-mail access, by the way, unless I pay for it at Kinko's or the public library. Kinko's is like an Internet café with copy machines.

I have some news that will surprise you, so sit down and take a deep breath. There's three parts. Here's the first: my part-time job I wrote you about, it's at the Pasadena Child Development Center on the Pasadena Technological Institute campus. I work there from eight thirty to two thirty, four days a week, with a group of eight babies. You know, of course, how much I love this kind of work, and the director of the center gave me the job when she saw my work record from home. Steve saw to it that I brought my transcripts along when we moved here in '82—he always looked ahead and wanted the best for me.

I'm enrolled in some refresher courses in child development

at our local community college. Most of what I learn, I already know from those early childhood courses I took in Bulawayo. Even with different cultural settings, infants and children all over the world follow pretty much the same patterns of development. But it fascinates me to learn the U.S. ways of bringing up kids and see the good and bad parts of that. We had good and bad parts the way we did it at home, too—I could go on about that!

But I'm far away from the second part of what I want to tell you. Your little Farai attends this child care center where I work. I've met Chipo once—after Hannah, our director, told her an African woman was on the staff, she came over to my building to see me. Farai's building is a fair distance from mine, of course, since he's four and I'm with the babies. But I've only seen her that one time, because she seems to want to chart her own course somehow. I guess it's as you told me: we of the older generation are kept at arm's length. But your young grandson was very friendly—he and I chatted a little in Shona, and he smiled a huge smile when I told him I knew you. He is a wonderful boy, Ruvimbo. You must be so proud of him.

My friend, here's the third thing, and it's very important. I know from one of the teachers who works with Farai's group that Tapiwa left Chipo last week. Farai continues to stay with her. It's known that Tapiwa has moved in with an American woman he met at the Pasadena Technological Institute. Lord knows what he can be thinking of! He and Chipo don't speak, except about Farai now and then. I think maybe this completely different place and culture, plus the pressure to make decent grades, has made Tapiwa a little crazy right now. We see it here from time to time. A woman from Australia told me a few years ago, "People go on walkabouts for a while." It happened back home in our village too, didn't it?

Anyway, I wonder if you could possibly scrape up the funds to come visit me for a few weeks here, and help Chipo. Of course, as you know, I don't have children of my own, so I haven't had personal experience like you, but I've worked with many families, and I feel sure that Chipo will welcome you. She's so isolated and hurt right now.

And it would be such a joy for me to see you again! We'll have to live simply, but I can stretch my quarters and meals to take care of you. I have a daybed as well as a pull-out sofa, so you can be comfortable nights. There's lots of great things to see and do in this part of the world too. Please come if you can. You can phone and leave a message for me at the infant building if it looks possible.

I hope you'll come!

Sekai

24

Observation Assignment, EC 240
Time and date: 12:30 p.m., Friday 1/15/99—transition into
nap time
Setting: fours room, PCDC
Description (brief): Slightly chilly, even indoors. Eighteen
children and five staff: Anne Williams and four other staff
Observer: Hannah Cooper
Number of pages: 2

Today I continue to observe the same group of four-year-
olds, but at a different hour. Five teachers are with eighteen
children, enjoying one of their several daily group meetings
together. Three or four at a time, all the children have used the
toilet and washed their hands. Now they're sitting on the soft,
worn carpet in the small book nook. The lead teacher, Anne,
is on a child-sized chair facing the children, her back to me.
With the group are three other staff members, each with a child
or two on their laps. Several pillows cushion the walls. This
reading nook's small enough that some part of everyone touches
some part of someone else. A fifth staff member, Tony, sets out

child-sized nap mats—forty-eight by twenty-four inches—in the next room. Each mat has its own sheet and blanket marked with a child's name, and most also have a special pillow or stuffed animal belonging to that child.

In a clear, gentle voice, Anne reads *Angus and the Cat,* the children's classic by Marjorie Flack. It's about a young Scots terrier, Angus, and a wary older cat. After initial cat hostilities, the cat and Angus end up sharing the same bowl of food.

Even the children who speak little English absorb each word and whimsical detail of the drawings. Every child here works to make friendships, and the simple events and feelings in the story speak straight to their experience.

The children are drowsy after their lunch, outdoor play, and story time. Anne calls their names, hugs each child one by one. They head for their mats, lie down and hug their stuffed animals, pull up their blankets, and close their eyes. Peaceful music plays softly. The entire group goes off to sleep while two staff members watch over them. It will be at least an hour before the first one wakens, and perhaps an hour and a half before all are up and ready again for snacks.

25

Harare
January 4, 1999

My Dear Sekai,

You are a true friend to invite me to share your place, and
I'm so grateful, too, that you're in the same part of the world as
Chipo and Farai and can give me their news. To answer your
invitation, *yes*! I found a way to pay for the air fare, round trip
from Harare to Los Angeles and back (will tell you *how* when
I see you—it's a story in itself, believe me). The ticket's secure,
but the date's not certain—some time this month, after the
eighteenth. I'll call you as soon as I know.
    In haste—Ruvimbo

26

"I brought this verse of Emily Dickinson's to read you," Sue Bowles told Phyllis Arden, her therapist—who was also a PCDC mom—one day early in January. And she recited:

> There's a certain slant of light,
> On winter afternoons,
> That oppresses, like the weight
> Of cathedral tunes.

"It's not that I miss Alan, exactly," she continued. "I just feel numb about him, numb about Sophie's death too." Numb. The word sounded forlorn between the two women. Their sessions were held in a small cottage behind Phyllis' home, a pleasant setting that seemed only to increase Sue's lethargy. Her body was planted in a soft chair, and her eyes were closed. She had seen Phyllis weekly since October when Alan left for South America. He was due to return at the end of this month, in time for Aaron's fifth birthday.

Moments of silence, one after another. Finally Sue spoke. "Just once I've been able to feel the hurt. It happened during the holidays, when Aaron and I were alone. We invited Farai

Moyo over to play, and it really helped. It's funny, but I only feel normal and maybe halfway happy when those two boys are together! ... But then the numbness set in again."

"What about William? You told me how alive you felt when you had sex with him last month. How does he fit into your feelings now?"

"Sex with William that one time brought me alive for a day or so, but we both knew it couldn't continue, and we've made sure not to let it happen again. He's still a good friend to Aaron and me. But this awful numbness overwhelms me so much of the time. It just goes on and on. And Phyllis, I still haven't been able to cry since Sophie's death. I know tears are in there somewhere, but they just won't come." Sue mustered a small smile.

"Tell me how you and Alan made the decision for him to leave even though you'd just lost your baby," Phyllis asked gently. She sat in the only chair in the room with no cushions or upholstery.

"Well, he had this once-in-a-lifetime research grant to go to the Galapagos and observe the tortoises—"

"I'm not a marine biologist, Sue. Tell me why that's important." Phyllis' soft voice interrupted Sue's words.

"Because ..." Sue sighed, a long, quiet exhalation, "... the concern about the tourist cruises there, that's why." She sounded dry, irritable. "Big boats aren't good for turtles, birds, marine life." She heard herself speaking as if by rote, and continued.

"And then"—her tongue sounded against her teeth for a second—"for Alan, of course it's his big chance to advance in his field. He'll write up his observations. Actually, he's very excited about a theory he has. And it's 'publish or perish,' you know, Phyllis."

No response. Finally Sue broke the long silence. "I know that might seem pretty far-fetched in the face of our Sophie's death in August."

"About Alan's trip right now, do you have any feelings besides acceptance?"

Sue shifted in her chair, crossed and uncrossed her legs. "I've asked myself that, but it seems like just *numb*'s all I feel, so much of the time."

Phyllis' fingers steepled in her lap as she gazed straight ahead out the window.

"During this week ahead, could you think a little about boundaries? I know you love Alan with all your heart, but you and he are two different people. And your needs are different." She paused. "Are you still not sleeping much?"

"I take the sleeping meds you prescribed—but not always. Scared of getting hooked, I guess. Last night I didn't take any. Hardly slept at all. I lay awake and fantasized."

"Fantasized? About what?" Phyllis' eyes gleamed at the hint of some fresh development in the stuck life of her client.

"Well, about Farai coming to live with Aaron and me. The three of us get along so well together, and I love to see Aaron so happy with him. I feel like Farai could bring me back to life—oh, I do know this is stupid, but that's what kept me awake last night all the same!" Sue sat up straight and looked into her therapist's eyes for a moment before subsiding again into the chair.

They had used up their fifty-minute hour. Sue let out another long sigh. Had she progressed at all in these therapy sessions? Everything seemed to move at a snail's pace, even her work with Phyllis.

27

Friday, January 8

"What on earth made you and Joan plan to have a *sheriff* come and talk to us, for God's sake?" Tony Gibson groaned as he lounged back in his beanbag chair. The beanbag groaned, too, under his corpulent form. Lead teacher Anne Williams presided, and Hannah lent support as the fours staff gathered for its weekly meeting, a few days before Sheriff Bronson's annual January visit.

Tony had creative ideas for activities with children but could often be unrealistic in implementing them, Hannah knew well. His teammates were frequently frustrated by his edgy, obscure communication style.

"I think it's a great idea," said Sandy. "Get 'em used to the idea, early on, that someone's out there they can trust besides their parents, someone they can go to if they're scared or lost."

Sandy was Tony's age, twenty-five, and worked half-time in the afternoons. Hannah saw in her a waif struggling to come to terms with her own difficult childhood, to appear mature and streetwise.

"Sandy, they can go to their mom or dad if they're scared, can't they? They're only four, after all, wouldn't they go to their own mom or dad if they were scared?" Tony asked.

"Hah. You're so innocent, Tony. It's because your mom and dad stayed together and you had a stable childhood. Most kids today are, like, on their own emotionally, from day one. Do you think these little guys are here with us instead of at home with Mom because their parents love them?" Sandy ran her hand fast through her spiky punk haircut.

"Sheriff Bronson comes every year, Tony," Hannah interjected. She tried to project across the decades to him: "It's really about giving them an intro to community. Victoria comes from the library, Fred from the fire department, Javier from the post office ..."

"Okay, I remember all that from grade school," Tony cut in. "A dentist came too. But at four years old! What can they get from it?"

Tony's exaggerated lounger pose irritated Hannah. She knew they had to take time for him to voice his doubts, and for Sandy to respond to him. From these precious interactions could come growth and understanding. If only they didn't have to consume so much time doing it though! It seemed as if the staff completely ignored the printed sheet they held in their hands, the agenda of items they themselves had requested the previous week. Instead, they had completely different and often unconscious agendas in their heads. Tony and Sandy seemed to think it a matter of freedom of speech to say whatever crossed their minds.

"Trust me, Tony," Sandy assured him. "You haven't heard Sheriff B. yet. When you do, you'll get it that he really knows kids. He has three or four at home, and he knows how to talk to them. Wait till you hear him."

"And another thing," Tony blared on, oblivious to

Sandy's annoyance, "how come we have a sheriff instead of a policeman? The kids would understand 'police' better than 'sheriff,' wouldn't they?"

This time Angie, filling in on Anne's team today for an absent staff member, attempted both to explain to and calm Tony. "I think it's because PTI's in an unincorporated area, Tony," she told him. "In this part of Pasadena we don't have police services. We're under the county, right, Hannah?"

Hannah nodded, adding that the children had never in her experience seemed confused by the difference between sheriff and police officer. She would talk with Sandy later about her own view that most of the children in their program were much loved, not victims of neglect as Sandy assumed.

Tony subsided, though his raised eyebrows spoke clearly: *I know a few things about the world of crime prevention.*

The staff meeting, held during nap time while the teachers kept one eye on the sleeping group of children in the next room, broke up a few moments later when the first child began to yawn and stir. There was no time to talk about Thomas Johnson, Hannah realized, though it was urgent. Anne hadn't had a chance to mention the important and confidential information that Thomas' parents had separated last weekend, and that a neighbor had called the sheriff's office during an argument at the Johnsons'.

Why did they never have enough time at staff meetings to talk together about important matters?

Always the urgent needs of the present seemed to break into their time together. It was like trying to change a tire on a moving car.

Hannah visualized a time when these meetings could be held in a civilized way, with adult-sized table and chairs, and coffee and snacks available. In this child care center of her dreams, plenty of paid time would exist for staff to consider and discuss all the necessary things and reach group decisions— time even to discuss fascinating ideas about children, like Erik

Erikson's eight stages of life. Erikson was one of Hannah's heroes, along with Maria Montessori, Abraham Lincoln, and Nelson Mandela.

Later Hannah would look back on this moment as one of relative peace. Sheriff Bronson, who came each year to talk with both groups of four-year-olds about proactive, nonviolent social strategies, would return very soon to the center because of a tragic death—possibly a murder.

28

Deputy Sheriff Patrick Bronson strode into the small room promptly Monday morning at ten o'clock as the children in the fours group finished their apple wedges. He wore full uniform: khaki pants and shirt and his shiny sheriff's badge on his brown jacket. His six-foot-three height loomed by contrast with the fours, though he was leaner than some of them. The female staff held him in admiration, and the men felt comfortable with him too; he had recently written a character reference for Alonzo, an afternoon staff member of this group. Bronson's gun rested in a holster out of sight under his arm beneath his jacket. Hannah had asked him to leave his billy club in the trunk of his official car.

"Hi, kids, it's good to see y'all again," he began, unaware that most of the children he'd seen in this room last year had moved on to kindergarten. "Ah'm Sheriff Bronson, and it's mah job to be there to help when help's needed. Some of you might've seen me on TV. Ah'm the good guy that chases the bad guys."

Hannah knew Bronson exaggerated his accent for the kids.

They loved it, and trusted the easygoing, warm persona he projected.

"Do you come for car accidents, Sheriff?" she asked, to start the questions flowing.

"Oh yes, Hannah, we help then. And sometimes a boy or girl gets lost in the parking lot or in a supermarket, and we help then too." Bronson grinned, and the children watched him, their usually restless bodies completely still and their eyes fastened on his person.

Kai boldly got up, went over to the sheriff, and stood directly before him, hands behind his back, staring intently.

"Where's your gun?" he demanded.

"Ah do have a gun," Bronson responded, "but we try never to use them if we can help it. We try to use our *words*. Like, if you took mah ball away from me, Ah'd maybe say to you, 'It's mah turn now. You can have a turn soon.' Or if you shoved me goin' out the door, Ah might say, 'Quit shovin'!' but Ah wouldn't shove you and Ah wouldn't pull out mah gun."

Kai shot back, "You killed anyone?"

Bronson dropped his easygoing manner and his accent and looked gravely into Kai's eyes. "No, buddy, I haven't had to do that, and I hope I never will."

Most of the teachers understood the ideas he presented, and they themselves consistently used them with the children at the center. The four- and five-year-old children knew them backward and forward. For example—Hannah smiled as she remembered this—four-year-old Ardis had seen Anne approaching in the play yard the previous week, and suddenly switched from pointing a wooden block at Adam and shouting, "Bang! You're dead!" to smiling sweetly at Anne, telling her, "This is my pretend camera and I'm taking Adam's picture."

Even at this age, the kids think broccoli and sharing are boring, and French fries and shoving are cool, Hannah mused—that whole thing of doing the opposite of what the adults tell you. The fun, bad-boy thing. But here was a manly adult who told them not to push and shove and urged them to use their words instead. *He* was credible.

She noticed that Thomas Johnson had hidden his head in Kathy's lap at the back of the group. His shoulders were tense, his body compacted. She knew why Thomas would be scared of their uniformed visitor.

"Would you all like to come outside and see mah sheriff's car?" Bronson asked, and most of the group jumped up instantly and headed for the door. There was no need to stop for jackets on this mild January morning; the eighteen children, accompanied by Sandy, Kathy, Howard, and Anne, spilled rapidly through the play yard and out the gate to the street. Bronson's black car, resplendent with its shiny trim, bore the gold-lettered words "Pasadena Sheriff's Department." Bronson unlocked it and opened all four doors wide. Some children took turns climbing in and out and over the seats while Kathy and Howard stood watchfully on the street side of the car. Others, safe on the sidewalk, stared at the rotating red and blue light on the roof.

"Are you okay with a really loud noise?" he asked them. "If you are, Ah'm going to turn on the siren, just for a second."

Cecily, Sarah, and some of the others squealed happily and covered their ears. Kai socked Craig, who passed on the shove to Song Lee. Bronson switched on the siren and immediately shut it off again, and the children froze to attention. Then, seeing no signs of fear in the group, he turned it on again, this time for several seconds.

After most of the children had tired of the patrol car experience—some, of course, would never get enough of it— Bronson led them back to their room. He passed around his handcuffs and fielded questions they now vied with each other to ask.

"But we don't use the cuffs very often," he reminded them. "These are mostly just on TV. Do you know how you can best help us do our job?" He lowered his voice to a whisper, and every child sat still and focused on his answer. "Listen to Anne and Kathy and Howard here," — he swiftly scanned the staff's name badges—"and listen to Mom or Dad when you're with them. They love you, they want what's best for you, you can count on them."

Hannah looked over at Sandy, whose eyes were fixed on Bronson's face. She actually nodded, confirming Bronson's words. Gone was her frequent cynical expression of doubt. And Hannah noted, too, that Thomas had wiggled into the front row. His plump body was sprawled out, one knee crossed over the other; his hands lay limp and open on his chest. His expression, like his body, was relaxed, in remarkable contrast to his earlier fear and misery. It appeared he'd lost his fear of uniforms, thanks to Bronson's visit. Score two for this handsome outsider.

She would ask Anne to make a note later in the day in Thomas' folder.

29

After his visit to the fours, Bronson stopped by Hannah's office.

He's really a most thoughtful, easygoing man, Hannah thought. *And it's kind of fun being on a first-name basis with an actual sheriff, even if it's childish to feel that way.*

Outside the lone window of her office, the oak branches swayed in a light wind. If you stood close to the window you could see a steady stream of traffic flowing below.

"Hannah, what's your relationship with PTI?" he asked her bluntly, his Southern drawl almost gone. "I'm asking because of that homeless man, the one campus security found in one of your play yards last fall. I noticed that it was Kevin Drabb, the PTI community rep, who called me about it, not you. And he did that maybe a week after the guy broke into your play yard. Can you shed any light?"

"Maybe a little, Patrick. About the homeless man, campus security makes a nightly check of PCDC, and when they found him, Kevin notified me the next morning, which I appreciated. Campus security had his name. I asked Kevin whether I could call you about it, and he said he'd prefer to do it himself. He probably thought it wasn't high priority, so didn't call you right away."

"Why would he prefer to call my office himself, instead of having you do it, do you think?"

Bronson's questions touched on a subject painful to Hannah, and she gathered her thoughts to give as clear a reply as possible.

"I'll try to make this short, Sheriff. Since PTI doesn't own the Center—we're a private nonprofit, with our own finances and board of directors—neither Kevin nor PTI legally has control of the center. Nothing in the center's bylaws or my contract mentions the community rep's existence. But ..."

"Of course he has control over the center, Hannah! It's just reality! After all, you serve mainly campus children—what did you tell me, eighty percent?—and you're located right on campus—on the fringe, but on campus! You even pay PTI some kind of token rent, don't you? How would PTI *not* have control?"

She drew herself up straight.

"I can only say it's never been spelled out. The center's independence is what's spelled out. We've begged PTI to incorporate us."

"And lose your precious independence?" His eyebrows rose as he gave her a sideways eye roll.

"Most of the center staff would gladly trade independence for pay scales and benefits equal to the classified staff at PTI. But PTI won't accept that expense. Or the liability."

Bronson sat up straight and stared, clearly interested in what she told him.

"It's a complex relationship we have, Patrick. Kevin does give us generous help when he can—prompt plumbing and electrical help, even some maintenance, and now and again a deluxe staff dinner, for instance."

"So?"

"So *that's* why he feels he can tell me, which he did only

a few weeks ago when he found out I'd called you to come talk to our children—that PTI would prefer I not call public agencies such as the sheriff's office, city hall for pest control, or the mayor's office, and of course not the *Daily Pasadena Press*. He specifically instructed me always to call him first for any public matters."

Bronson's eyes widened. "Even in an emergency, Hannah?"

"Well, of course we can dial nine-one-one in a medical emergency or a fire. But for anything except those, Drabb has clearly instructed me to go through him."

Hannah's phone rang, and she spoke briefly with a parent who wanted to enroll a child at the center. She gave the parent the date of the next orientation for those interested in enrollment, took the name and address of the caller, and promised to send an invitation with details of time and place. Then, as if no interruption had occurred, she turned back to Bronson and resumed.

"Geared as I am to community involvement, like working with other centers on early childhood causes or generating newspaper publicity during the Week of the Young Child, it's been hard for me to play along with PTI's agenda. But the aid PTI gives us is extremely important to us."

Bronson stood, paced around the office once, and sat down again. A delicious smell wafted up the stairs from below—James' special won-ton soup, Hannah knew.

"I'd have to go back twenty-five years and tell you the history of this center, Patrick, and the founding mission, to help you understand my concern over some of what's happening now in terms of PTI controlling certain center policies—but I've probably told you enough for one day." She smiled at him.

"I'll just say that I've seen other child care centers suddenly shut down by the hospital or industry that had supported them," she continued, "and I never want that to happen to us." Her voice shook and she paused a moment, then gave Bronson a sharp look. "I wouldn't tell you all this if I didn't feel I could trust you."

"Well, it must be a bind for you sometimes," he told her, "but I guess administration's always a tightrope. That's why so many people don't want that kind of responsibility, right?"

He thought a moment. "I didn't realize you were on such a tight leash. How would you want this to play out in the future, Hannah?"

"My vision for the center? That PTI accept it for what it is, a nationally accredited agency governed by standards of excellence that PTI knows nothing about, since it has no department of child development and no desire to form one. PTI could fully fund our center and pay rates to our staff similar to those it pays its classified staff—health and retirement benefits included. The tuition brought in by the center would reimburse the institute by at least fifty percent, and the institute could count on space availability for PTI children. It would be a loss for the center—of diversity and community enrichment, not to mention community support—but it could then agree to no longer serve non-PTI children." She found herself breathless as she spilled this out.

"'Standards of excellence' sounds pretty lofty, Hannah. Are they spelled out someplace?"

"They are indeed, Patrick. We're accredited by the National Association for the Education of Young Children, a professional organization with close to a hundred thousand members. Its headquarters are in DC, and there are active state and regional chapters as well."

She could sense Bronson's waning interest, observing his restless legs and shifts in his chair, and for the thousandth time she wished she could make quality child care as thrilling to others as it was to her.

He gave her a look of understanding. "Going back to what you said earlier, I see why you didn't call me about the homeless man in your play yard last fall, all right!—though I still have questions about him. What do you think he was doing there? Was it a one-time thing? Have you or any of your staff received weird phone calls? Or any of the parents at your Center? Have you heard of or felt any kind of danger, Hannah?"

Her throat tightened on hearing his questions. "No, really not," she responded, "nothing I can think of."

"Okay, then I'll see you in February when I talk to the other group, like we agreed."

She thought he looked relieved as he said good-bye with a smile. Was it because she'd lectured him? He *had* asked her about her vision for the Center, after all.

30

Pasadena
Tuesday, January 12, 1999

It was a reception room like any other: nondescript beige chairs, a table with dull magazines about boats, and nautical photographs on the walls. Maureen and Hannah sat waiting to speak with State Assemblyman Harold Moore about required ratios of teachers to children. Moore officially returned to Pasadena twice a year from Sacramento and saw his constituents then. Unofficially, he returned most weekends to his Pasadena family on North Madison Avenue.

AB 469 was due to come up on the Assembly floor, and the two women wanted his vote. They received weekly information and direction from a statewide network, and from their professional organization's lobbyist in Sacramento.

Hannah's advocacy activities sprang from her gut desperation about the thousands of children in their crucial formative years who don't receive the services and tender, enlightened love she felt to be every child's birthright. Her inner urgency about this sometimes sabotaged her presentations, so she had chosen Maureen as her advocacy partner.

Hannah saw her friend as "Maureen the articulate." At one time Maureen had directed a local child care center, but now she headed the Child Development Department at City College. Hannah felt lucky to have Maureen on her center's personnel committee as well. The two women made a good advocacy team. Hannah tended to be serious and precise. Her friend was smart and funny, so people didn't immediately "get" Maureen's serious passion to make a difference for children. Her charm and wit dazzled them, allowing her to make important points and raise crucial issues.

Both women wore suits, bright blouses, medium-heeled shoes, and hose; their hair was brushed and neat, and they were nicely made up. This was Maureen's everyday work garb, while Hannah usually wore pants, T-shirts, and jackets with clogs or sandals at the center—lipstick if she remembered. Maureen, in her early thirties, was slender, with straight blond hair. Her gray eyes sparkled.

Hannah had taken a break from the center that afternoon to join Maureen. The pair did these advocacy calls fairly often, though this would be the first one with Moore, who was known in their circles as a conservative. "And not the kind who wants to conserve children, either!" they'd been told. So they'd prepared carefully for this visit—boned up on the latest research on quality child care outcomes, checked Moore's dismal voting record, and sent him a packet of information beforehand. They were loaded for bear.

Moore's receptionist spoke anxiously into her phone. "Honey, you know I can't come home for another three hours ... how long have you felt this way?"

"You *what?* Sweetie, take a Tylenol right now, and try to drink at least one glass of water. Where's Alyssa? Not *there?* Listen, call Grace next door and let her know how you feel. Ask her to call me after she's seen you, okay?"

"How old is your child?" Maureen gently asked the receptionist after she'd completed the phone call.

"Nine. She's in fourth grade. No room in the after-school program. I pay the sitter good money, but she hasn't shown up today. I've *got* to find someone reliable." She pulled her shoulders together, exhaled, and gave a little laugh. "You want the job?"

Her buzzer sounded, and Moore's staccato voice commanded, "Send 'em in, Roberta."

Maureen and Hannah entered Moore's office and crossed a seemingly endless distance over thick, springy pale blue carpet. They seated themselves in comfortable brown leather chairs across from his desk.

The desk's big enough to serve eight, thought Hannah.

A computer keyboard stood at the ready on a credenza angled to Moore's left. On the desk itself were only a pen, today's *Los Angeles Times,* and a photograph of a woman, a little girl, and two young teen-aged boys, all smiles, with perfect teeth. A few books—legal texts, Hannah thought—stood on otherwise empty shelves to the left. The large window in front of them was sealed shut, muffling traffic two stories below on Pasadena's main street. They were at the east end of town, and to the north they could see tall palms swaying against the metallic, smoggy sky. They knew the San Gabriel Mountains were out there too, but smog completely enveloped them this afternoon.

Moore didn't rise. He wore a blue shirt and dark red tie; his navy slacks barely visible from where they sat. He looked to be in his fifties. He had an ample torso, and thinning, well-combed hair partially covered his small head. His narrow lips looked capable of indifference. Pale blue eyes watered beneath shaggy eyebrows.

The eyebrows are lasting better than the hair, Hannah thought.

She tended to be nervous in the presence of power in spite of the workshops she'd led and the mock press conferences she'd taken part in during her advocacy training. So she made herself visualize the last time she'd stood on the capitol steps in Sacramento with other child care workers—and felt stronger.

"So ladies, what brings you here today?" he greeted them in an affable tone. His use of the word "ladies" made Hannah's stomach tighten. She felt treated as though she and Maureen wore flowered hats and were standing with him at an afternoon tea party in a garden—while he made deliberately meaningless conversation.

"It's about AB four sixty-nine, Mr. Moore," Maureen began. She chose not to start the interview on a negative note by pointing out that they'd written him ahead of the meeting and had already sent him the relevant materials. If he'd done his job, he would have read what they'd sent and been ready to discuss it.

"As you know" (*did* he know?), "AB four sixty-nine would lower the required number of teachers for groups of two-year-old children.

"If the bill goes through, *one* teacher could find herself working alone with *twelve* children who are only two years old. At present, *two* teachers are required for that number, up to two and a half years old."

"So—is there a big difference between two-year-olds and two-and-a-half-year-olds?"

"Yes, Mr. Moore." Hannah tried to think of something he might easily understand. "For one thing, a two-year-old's slightly more likely to be in diapers than a two-and-a-half-year-old."

Moore winced, as if a momentary whiff of ripe diaper had reached him.

Maureen nodded. "The cognitive and physical difference between a two-year-old and a two-and-a-half-year-old is significant, Mr. Moore. Twelve two-and-a-half-year-olds to one teacher, which the law now permits, is already unwise. Twelve *two-year-olds* to one teacher is beyond unwise. In plain English, it would be warehousing the children."

Moore's eyes glazed over as he heard these numbers. His attitude was apparent: Hannah felt him perceiving herself and her friend as suffragettes, or perhaps ladies from the Women's Christian Temperance Union, and she struggled not to yield her identity to what she felt was his image of her. She dug in her bag. "I have with me another of the information packets we sent you last week, Representative Moore, if you want to see the bill and background information."

He took the packet she offered him across the expanse of his desk. "Oh yes, now I remember," he muttered as he quickly scanned the first paragraph of the bill and a brief summary of the well known Perry Street study. The study's thorough dollars-and-cents analyses were based on forty years of research on groups of children in Ypsilanti, Michigan, who received quality child care. These children's outcomes in high school and later were compared to the outcomes of control groups from similar backgrounds who did not receive the same level of quality care. The results were clear: quality early childhood education saves society many hundreds of thousands of dollars in terms of need for public services later—services that range from special education and teen pregnancy care to drug rehab and prison. The research is impeccable and the study universally respected.

Moore looked up. "Well, ladies, I'll certainly give this my utmost consideration. Our time has run out, but is there anything else you'd like to discuss? Oh—let me give you a copy of my voting record." He rummaged in a file drawer to his right and handed them each a four-by-eight-inch card, printed in bright blue letters and with red headings. "Here it is. You can see that I've consistently supported prison improvements and building new prisons. I want to keep this community and the state of California safe for our children." He beamed at them.

Hannah was speechless. She wanted to scream, "Don't you

get it? Quality care for children significantly *reduces* crime and the number of people sent to jail!"

Moore stood, walked around his desk toward them, and extended his hand first to Hannah, then Maureen. Clearly, he was about to usher them out genially, when his phone rang.

As he listened, he turned pale and sagged back into his chair, then asked a few terse questions, looked relieved, and assured his caller that he would be home shortly. To Hannah's astonishment, he looked right into her eyes, then Maureen's, one human being connecting to two human beings, and when he spoke his voice had shifted from its former suave impersonality.

"Ladies, that was my wife. A couple of kids threatened our middle child at knife point this afternoon on his way home from school. He's okay, she says. Our neighborhood on North Madison Avenue isn't safe anymore. Our home there, it was my folks' home, it used to be completely safe when I was growing up. Now we're looking to move to a gated community. I just can't see how these preschools you talked about will change anything. Frankly, it's too late already."

He stopped, perhaps realizing how unprofessional he sounded. Hannah suddenly understood that she might not be the only one to falter sometimes. She wanted to let go of her frustration and give some comfort, but the right words wouldn't come. She and Maureen both pressed his hand, murmured sympathetic words, and encouraged him to get home to his family. The three went to his outer office together. Moore told Roberta to close the office early, and left.

The receptionist joined Maureen and Hannah a moment later outside in the hall as they waited for the elevator. "You were good. I listened on the intercom. Please don't stop." She pressed a card into their hands. "And if you hear of a decent after-school program with a space, please call me."

In the elevator the women realized they'd connected with their man. Slow work, advocacy. Actually it was the phone call from his wife more than anything they'd said that helped them connect. But maybe he'd remember and give them his vote. Or was it already too late for him to believe that anything could be done?

31

From Hannah's desk, to Staff and Parents, Tuesday evening, 1/12/99:

PCDC Panel For Parents, Tuesday, January 26
7:00 PM
Child Care Provided

As many of you have already heard, PCDC suffered a sad and shocking loss today. Angie Masson arrived early at the Center to arrange her classroom for the morning and discovered that Henry, one of our pet rabbits, had been killed. Bushes were trampled and blood smeared on the play house and some of the children's play equipment. Angie called me promptly, and I was able to clean up the damage before the children arrived.

At circle time (as you know, the children and their teacher sit in a circle every morning to discuss group plans and feelings, to play games sometimes, and to make group decisions) Joan, Angie, and the rest of the staff in the fours group talked with the children about Henry. We all knew what needed to be done: give the children time to think and talk about their feelings. So

Angie and Joan rearranged their morning events to allow plenty of time to talk and share.

Some of the children wanted to put a padlock on the rabbit cage. One or two wanted a "bunny guard" to sleep in front of the cages overnight. The other bunny, Mabel, got more than her usual petting and fresh lettuce, and Angie followed through on the children's concern by installing a padlock before the end of the day.

Campus Security will patrol our play yards twice each night for the present, rather than just once as they normally do. Sheriff Bronson will be part of a panel about security measures here a week from next Tuesday evening, January 26, as well. The older children are already familiar with Sheriff Bronson, as he comes each year to talk with them about what sheriffs do in our community. He'll be joined by Ed Black of campus security, and Phyllis Arden, who's a therapist and mother of Tim in the fours. If you have concerns about this matter, plan to attend and bring your questions. Child care will be provided. Meantime, please feel free to share your questions or concerns with your child's teacher, or with me—Hannah Cooper, director.

32

Thursday, January 14, 1999

A skinny youth with shaggy blond hair, George Vincent sat in the back room of the Computer Shack, tinkering with a printer. On his screen were the manufacturer's instructions. Of course the printer, a year and a half old, was hopelessly out of date, but the Shack catered to owners who didn't want to update their machines. They just wanted them fixed. Or anyway, that's what he'd heard the old gal say when she brought it in this morning.

"Not on warranty?" she'd squawked. "I can't believe it! My washing machine's over eighteen years old, and never a problem! What's happened to manufacturer accountability?"

Ben, his boss, familiar with sentiments like these, was willing to come halfway to his customer. "I know, Mrs. Cooper, it's a different world, isn't it?" he crooned to her. "And the youngsters just don't get it. But we'll try to do the best we can for you and keep the price reasonable."

He'd calmed her down—George could tell by a change in tone—though clearly she didn't know her output tray from her status panel. "Well thanks, Ben. I hate to keep bothering you like this," she told him as he gave her a receipt for the printer. "How soon do you think you could have it ready? I'm hamstrung at the office without it."

Again he soothed her. "You're one of our regulars, Ms. Cooper. We'll try for tomorrow, after four p.m. Will that be okay?"

"It'll have to be, Ben. My home printer works—knock on wood—so if I have print jobs today I'll take them home with me from work. See you tomorrow."

George heard the door close behind her brisk step. Where did he know her from? He knew he had some kind of connection to her. It related to Elaine. But Elaine didn't have kids, so how—

Then he remembered. The black guy. The one that moved in with Elaine last month, the bastard. The one with the fancy scholarship and the swagger. His name was Tapu? Teepee? He had a kid, didn't he? Right, and the kid went to Ms. Cooper's daycare; he would bet on it.

A bitter chuckle erupted as he recalled how little interest Elaine had in children. She must have to put up with the kid sometimes now. Served her right!

It made him so mad last spring, the way Elaine right away would get the theory behind their class assignments. Seemed like he could always get the tech but never the theory. He'd failed his courses at PTI that semester. And then she'd put him out, said he got in the way of her life, her studies. Who did she think she was, anyway?

And who did he think *he* was? He'd been a graduate student with a fine career ahead of him, everyone seemed to think, as a teacher, or maybe doing pure science in a big commercial lab somewhere. Hell, his mother had certainly thought so. He hadn't told her yet that he'd dropped out.

Actually, he wasn't exactly a dropout; he'd been told by his faculty advisor that his scholarship wouldn't be renewed; it hadn't been a decision he'd made on his own. He hadn't told his mother he worked full time at the Shack now either. He felt too mixed up about the change to put a good front on it.

And he hated it when these kinds of thoughts wormed their way into his head.

He cleaned the inside of the printer, inserted one of the shop cartridges, then closed the cover and put some paper in the tray. He connected the printer to the shop computer and pressed the keyboard print command. It worked: a sheet of manufacturer's hieroglyphics emerged cleanly from the back of the printer. He gave the print command again, using the mouse this time. Once more, success.

Then he heard it. The door in the front of the shop opened, and Ben's greeting to the person or persons who entered sounded startled, fearful. "What do you want? We don't keep money in the shop," George heard Ben say.

"We are not wishing to harm you in any way," a British-sounding male voice responded. "We are looking for service on our cell phone. Do you repair cell phones as well as computers?"

We. So more than one person was talking to Ben. George got up quickly and moved to the open doorway between the repair area and the shop in front, cordless phone in hand, ready to call the sheriff's office if necessary.

Three black men, two young and one older and shorter, dressed in, what did they call them? dashookis?—those loud, loose shirts with no buttons—stood quietly across the counter from Ben. The taller ones resembled Elaine's lover, about Teepee's age and lean and fit, like him. They seemed comfortable in their skin, like Teepee, or whatever his name was. George felt rage rising, quickening his perceptions, and his hands trembled. Who did they think they were?

Ben had regained his calm. "Sure, we work on cell phones too. George, can you talk to these gentlemen?" he called, and George entered the shop, still holding his own phone.

"I hear no signal," the older man spoke. "Can you be of

help?" His words were courteous, but George thought he heard an edge of threat.

Just then Ben's wife pulled up in the loading space in front of the shop, blew her horn, and gestured to Ben to come outside. Maya used a walker to get around, but she could still drive. Ben stood up stiffly and went out to her, leaving the front door of the store open.

George tried to speak calmly. He asked the shorter man for his phone, looked at it, then plugged it in and tested it behind the counter. He made sure to face his customers as he did this. The phone made no sound. He inserted a shop battery, tested again, and the phone crackled to life.

"All you need's a new battery," he told the man. "We do mostly repairs here, not sales—"

The older man stiffened, and the two younger ones immediately pulled themselves more erect.

"But we do carry a few items for sale," he added quickly. "I'll see if we have a battery for this phone. I think we might," he continued. He wished Ben would return so he could look in the drawers behind him without turning his back to the men. He rummaged in the drawer in front of him, which contained only a phone directory and some triplicate order forms, as he well knew. He glanced out through the door. Maya's car pulled away from the curb, and Ben turned to cross the sidewalk and re-enter the shop. George swiveled halfway around to look in the drawer behind him yet still keep an eye on the men.

"You do not know where the batteries are?" the older man asked. George was saved from replying by Ben's return. He turned fully around then, found the right battery in its plastic bubble, and asked the man if he would like to buy it for twenty-eight dollars plus tax.

The three men spoke briefly together in their unintelligible tongue, then the older man nodded yes, asking, "And also, could you please install this new battery?" He pulled out a wallet, removed two crisp twenty dollar bills from it, and handed them to George on his open right palm. Then he resumed his earlier, easier stance, as did his companions. George rang up the sale, laid the change on the counter, then opened the plastic bubble and installed the battery while the three waited quietly.

"We are grateful for your assistance." The older man glanced at both Ben and George as he spoke. He took the phone from George, thanked him again, and headed for the front door, his companions behind him. At the doorway, all three paused and looked back toward George. "Good-bye," they almost sang, the "good" half an octave higher than the "bye."

"What the hell was that all about?" George asked Ben when the door closed behind the three men.

"You mean the good-bye? I'm not sure, but I know a lot of Africans speak English with a British accent. Didn't England own part of Africa at one time?" Ben scratched his head. "I know when I was in England during World War Two people always said good-bye when they left a shop. Funny custom. By the way, did those guys say anything while I was out front with Maya?"

George didn't answer. He seemed down, Ben thought, preoccupied about something. The guy was a whiz at repairing computers, though. Not a surprise when you thought about it. Anyone bright enough to get into PTI was *really* bright, Ben knew. Even if George hadn't graduated, he was bright all right.

33

"Hannah, here's what I want to ask you. Do you understand what's in this for Joan?" Mary had ordered her breakfast and now spoke seriously to her friend. She kept her voice low even in the nearly empty café.

Hannah gazed at her friend, eyes wide with puzzlement. "No, I truly don't get it. What benefit can she possibly get from stirring up all this trouble and negativity?"

"Face it, Hannah, some staff are just high-maintenance. Their preferred mode? Crisis to crisis. They get their kicks out of grief and stress—and if none is around, they'll manufacture it. It's their life blood. Where I work, we call them chaos junkies." Mary giggled in a way that invited Hannah to join her.

"But it's so counterproductive!" Their voices contrasted, Hannah realized, hers shrill while Mary's was low and soothing.

"As director, you're supposed to see it coming and head it

off before it gets blown out of proportion." Their waiter refilled their cups and set breakfast before them.

"You make it sound easy. Whatever happened to trusting people to act decently, do what they say they will, and keep their feelings balanced most of the time?" Hannah had never heard herself sound so querulous.

"I never called it easy. Let me tell you about the sabotage one of our supervisors is trying to wreak upon our skin care line even as we speak!" Mary recounted a bittersweet, partly funny tale about a woman on her staff who manufactured rumors, cried righteous crocodile tears, and incited coworkers to take up arms.

Hannah relaxed and laughed. "It's funny when *I* don't have to deal with it!" She blew out a long breath. "Thanks, Mary, I needed that!"

"Hannah, you have such high ideals for human relationships! Sometimes they just go wrong, and harden that way. Things can't always turn out the way you want. You've got to come on out of your ivory tower and *deal* with this woman, Hannah, or I warn you, she'll cause even greater havoc at your center than she has already!" Exasperation mixed with affection in Mary's tone.

"But," she continued, "you, my dear, are doing something so important in the world—*nothing's* more important than work with young families."

Warmth coursed unexpectedly through Hannah's body. She picked at the raisins in her bowl, and brightened.

"Next week I'll only tell you the fun stories about work, I promise."

"You have my permission to tell me the problems," said Mary. She tried to look dead solemn, then broke into laughter. "Just not about Joan! Her antics set my teeth on edge."

As they left the coffee shop together she put her arm around Hannah. "Want to see *Sleepless in Seattle* tonight with Bill and me? It's showing again at the Colorado. We didn't see it the first time round; did you?"

A night out at a funny, romantic movie would definitely be restoring. Hannah gave herself a shake and told herself she'd surely earned it.

34

Monday, January 18

How good it felt to be meeting in the evening, thought Hannah, even though part of her begrudged the time. Over a simple supper at Mark and Cindy Morrison's home, they would be able to focus and be assured of both privacy and freedom from the constant interruptions at the center. She'd bought a large plastic box of sushi in the morning and kept it in the office refrigerator as her contribution to the meal. Sushi is expensive, but she'd had no time to make it herself the night before at home. In a former life she'd loved to cook adventurously, with sushi as one of her specialties.

An accountant, Mark represented parents on the personnel committee, and Hannah was happy to have him as a colleague. He was friendly, mature, objective, and committed to sticking to whatever question the committee might address and finding a reasonable solution in as short a time as possible. In other words, he was a grown-up. She remembered when he and Cindy had brought her home-grown roses after her dearly loved cat Cotati was run over and killed.

Mark's fourth child, Sarah, was in Joan's fours class. Cindy worked full time as a nurse. Their home, busy and untidy, always appeared to Hannah to run peacefully. Mentally she compared it to her own home when her four children were young. Hannah marveled at Cindy and Mark's strong partnership and effective parenting.

When Maureen Brady arrived and sank gratefully into the Morrisons' comfortable armchair with a few pieces of sushi and a glass of iced tea beside her, Mark called the meeting to order.

"As you know, we're here to discuss a very sensitive issue, about Joan Nefas, teacher of one of the fours groups," he began, "and the possibility of Joan's termination. You've read the documentation on Joan's job performance that we asked Hannah a month ago to compile from her records. Since you received it, we've had a further incident, which is the reason Hannah asked for, and I called, this emergency meeting.

"But first, let's informally check our impressions of Joan's performance, both from the documentation and our personal interactions with her. If it's all right with you, I've asked Cindy to take notes while we brainstorm here. Everything we say, of course, is confidential. Are you both okay with this?"

Hannah well knew how gossip could spread at the center, like water gushing from a hydrant, but she also knew that both Cindy and Mark were discreet, mature, and ethical, and Maureen was a trusted friend and professional, so she nodded agreement.

"Let's begin with the positives," Maureen opened the discussion. "We all know how well liked and trusted Joan has been among many of the center parents who know her. We've noticed a slackening this year, but in the past her classroom has been at least passably managed. Joan's well known for spending hours counseling with parents, especially those new to parenting and new to the Center. We also know some parents strongly dislike her, more than any of our other lead teachers."

"All true," said Mark. "Andrew asked for this evaluation because he received several serious complaints from parents of children in Joan's group—which Hannah has worked on with Joan—and our personnel committee has supported Hannah in this because of Joan's potential. But now we have something much worse to deal with. Hannah, would you share this?"

Hannah spoke sorrowfully. "Joan twisted a child's wrist today to get him to come inside at nap time," she said. "Two staff members saw it happen, and came immediately to me about it. Last month a parent hinted he had seen a similar incident, but when I asked him to sign a statement about it, he refused, said maybe he'd exaggerated what he saw. The wrist-twist's why I asked for this meeting tonight."

It hurt Hannah to bring this out to Mark and Maureen. Twisting a child's wrist sounds so dreadful. The killer phrase in her world was *child abuse*, although those words cover an immense range of behaviors, from a light tap on a child's fully clothed bottom to shaking a child. The words have instant, universal shock power, the one thing people can always understand—or think they can.

Maureen and Mark understood these things, and had compassion, though all at the meeting were clear in their agreement with the legal requirement that a teacher who inflicts pain on a child—pain of any kind, physical or mental—must be fired.

"We know what this means," said Mark, shaking his head. "By law, Joan must be terminated—it's out of our hands. In a climate of trust such as we have at the center, everyone will be shocked and angry, and of course the children in her class will be affected. Many of the parents too—"

"Though I think the wrist-twist incident will be known to most of the parents in Joan's class by now," Maureen interrupted, "and most of them will feel that she should be dismissed."

Hannah felt terrible; she had supplied the evidence to the committee that would get Joan fired. This would go on Joan's record with the state of California, and Joan would not be able to find another job in the field. She also would not qualify for unemployment assistance, and like most child care workers, Joan lived from paycheck to paycheck.

"This will be a real bind for Hannah," said Maureen. "Remember, neither Hannah nor our committee is legally permitted to tell anyone other than Joan the reason for her dismissal. That law's supposed to protect Joan, but in a small community like ours it will look as if we've acted unjustly and then tried to protect ourselves by refusing to give information. Joan will be hurt and furious, and she'll try to stir up staff and parent support."

Indeed, the fabric binding this community of children, parents, and teachers together was woven out of mutual trust and affection. People shared confidences, food, books, understanding, car rides, and child care. They lent money. It felt safe to trust. Now the fabric would have an ugly tear in it. Everyone would feel the hurt. But Joan's physically hurting a child was now documented, and the course of action unavoidable.

"How best can we go about this?" asked Maureen. "Our board president must be present for the termination interview, and Andrew's first available time's late afternoon this Friday. A Friday dismissal interview's a good idea, I think, giving Joan the weekend to get her things moved out of the center. This also gives Hannah time to search for an interim sub."

"That sounds wise to me," Hannah said, "but I wonder about the four days between now and Friday. I can't have Joan with the children, given the reason for her dismissal. If I tell her she's to take the rest of the week off and come in to meet with us Friday afternoon, she'll know immediately what it's about and will likely resort to gathering support from certain parents and teachers."

"Judging from the policies in our firm," Mark offered, "you do have to go ahead and risk that."

"We're not required to inform her that the meeting's about termination," said Maureen. "We can simply say that our committee has asked for a meeting Friday, and that she's relieved of her duties for the rest of the week, with pay."

Their agreement complete, Mark made the phone call to Joan in the presence of the group—clear and businesslike, forestalling any discussion. The four sat in silence for a few moments when it was over.

Then Cindy ventured, "With three or four others on the staff in Joan's group, these next four days shouldn't be too difficult, should they?"

"It won't be easy, but Angie's a strong teacher, and so are Kathy and the others on that team. I think we can manage," Hannah responded.

They had no idea how difficult the managing would be.

35

Tuesday, January 19

"It's so good to be here with you, Sekai. It's summer at home and winter here, but January in Pasadena feels almost as warm as Harare right now! And I'm so confused about the day! It was Tuesday when I left, and you say it is still Tuesday?" A rich chuckle accompanied Ruvimbo's words.

Sekai had prepared a simple meal of soup and salad, and her friend Ruvimbo had exclaimed over the variety of fresh vegetables and leafy greens. Now Sekai put sheets, blanket, and pillow on a chair for her friend. She was small and quick, light-skinned. Her face changed expressions rapidly, and she talked and laughed a lot. She opened two bottles of beer, and the two women sat on the sofa, filled with the pleasure of their reunion after so many years.

"So now that you've caught your breath from your long trip here, let me tell you the little I know about Chipo and Farai, Ruvimbo. And then you should lie down and sleep for as long as you possibly can."

"Sleep! I've been awake for forty-eight hours, but I'm so

excited I don't feel sleepy at all! But of course I want to hear about Chipo. Tell me about her please, and about Farai. Is she all right? Has anything changed since you wrote?"

"Not much has changed as far as I know—Tapiwa's still with the American woman, and Chipo and Farai get by the best they can with the little money Tapiwa gives her. Farai does have his tuition paid at the center—it's part of Tapiwa's fellowship. Chipo may be able to get some kind of work, but she'll have to take cash wages."

"Because why?"

"Because her visa status makes it illegal to work here."

"Chipo should just come home with Farai!" Ruvimbo burst out.

"*Ndapota*, she's not able to think clearly right now, from what I hear. She just goes from day to day. She hates Tapiwa for what he's done, but she can't believe their marriage is over and she and Farai are on their own."

"He's just dropped right out of their life? Completely?"

"Once in a while Tapiwa does pick up Farai from the center in the evening and bring him home to Chipo. Days, she looks for work cleaning houses. It's so tough, my heart goes out to her. Ruvimbo, she needs her mother. Why don't you call her right now?" Sekai reached for her center directory and found Chipo's number.

"I see a notation that this number is a pay phone near her housing unit They save money that way. Go ahead, call your daughter."

Ruvimbo did as Sekai counseled. Haltingly, she punched in the numbers. She heard ringing, but no answer. Her shoulders sagged as she looked at her friend. She rang the number a second time.

"My hands are shaking. Please, you try." She handed over the phone.

Sekai looked up the number again and punched it in. No answer.

Ruvimbo considered, head to one side. She spoke tearfully. "Sekai, do you think I could see Farai without him knowing? I'm so hungry to lay eyes on him! After I've seen him, then I'll be able to think about the best way to make contact with Chipo—but I just have to see him first."

Sekai looked with love and empathy at her friend. Many a night during Steve's life, and even more since his death, she had shed tears over not being a mother herself. She felt she thoroughly understood Ruvimbo's wish to see Farai, to drink him in through her eyes before actually being with him and his mother.

"Ruvimbo! You haven't changed a bit! Always you follow your heart! Married young, had your child young—though we thought sixteen old back then, didn't we? Now you're in America just to see your grandson! But yes, if you think you can contain yourself—"

"Contain myself?"

"I'll sit with you in the car tomorrow, Wednesday, after closing time, across the street from one of the center buildings. An outdoor pizza stand is nearby where the parents can take their kids before going home. I've often seen Tapiwa buy pizza for Farai before taking him back to Chipo's. It'll be dark by then, but the stand is lit up, and you can watch and get at least a glimpse of him. But Ruvimbo, you have to understand—"

"What?"

"You'll want to leap out of my car and cover him with kisses, snatch him into the car. I know you! You'll lose it!"

"Lose what?"

"Losing it means you burst into tears and lose control, my friend," Sekai explained. "And most grandmas would do the same! But you can't do that, Ruvimbo. First off, from what you've told me, you'd be in deep trouble with Chipo. And for me, I'd probably lose my job for setting you up. They'd call it kidnapping, and that's a serious crime. It would be very hard to explain. Your accent would make it even worse. Trust me, I know what I'm talking about! You'd likely be jailed, at the very least, and deported in a hot second—like the next day."

"Well, I see what you're saying, and you're right—it'll be hard to just sit still and look. But I promise you I will. Then, after I've seen him, I'll call Chipo—that won't be easy either— and we'll go from there. I promise, Sekai."

She yawned hugely in spite of herself as she laid her head on the sofa pillow. The two friends made up the sofa with the sheets and blanket from the chair. "I feel as if I could sleep for twenty-four hours, even though I'm so excited," Ruvimbo whispered, and she curled up, closed her eyes, and breathed deep.

Sekai turned out all but one dim light and left her friend to her jet-lagged sleep. It was early, only eight o'clock, and she wasn't due at work until eight thirty the next morning. In her small bedroom she turned on her little black-and-white TV at low volume and lay as in a warm cocoon full of thoughts about her friend, until she, too, drifted into sleep.

In the morning she waited until eight, then gently woke Ruvimbo with a cup of steaming coffee. "More coffee and bread are on the table for you," she told her. "I'll be back after two. When it gets dark, around five thirty, we'll drive over to the pizza stand. My house is your house! Be at home, my friend. Maybe sleep some more." And she tiptoed out, headed for the center.

For the most part, it was a happy place to work, almost a second home, she thought. Most of the teachers and aides felt the same way, even after the scary rabbit killing last week.

36

Wednesday, January 20

A few short blocks from PTI, the Panda All You Can Eat presented itself in stunning white and chrome: shiny white tile floor, white Formica table tops. No music sounded, but scraping chairs and intermittent metallic clatter from the kitchen provided a comfortable sound base. The doors were already open at eleven that morning, and three women, PTI secretaries on an early lunch hour, enjoyed today's special: vegetable fried rice with sweet and sour pork.

When the three men—two tall, appearing to be in their twenties, and one older, shorter man—strode in that Wednesday, they caused an immediate stir even before one of them spoke in a warm, clipped accent. Their dashikis flowed almost neon bright against their blue-black skin, and their even teeth and fingernails shone. The two younger men looked extraordinarily fit—lean, muscled arms, high cheek bones, inquisitive, perceptive eyes. They gazed around, taking in the square white room, the buffet of chow mein, vegetable fried rice, sweet and sour pork, garlic eggplant, and beef broccoli.

They burst into delighted laughter, seemingly full of childlike pleasure and amazement at being here in this place, smelling these delicious smells. The secretaries exchanged glances and fell silent. Quietly, one of the women opened the cellophane wrap on her fortune cookie, removed the strip of white paper, and perused the contents. "You are a wise financial planner," she read to herself, laughed silently, and handed it to her friend.

The oldest of the three men stepped to the counter, where a teenaged server awaited his order. He carefully read the overhead signs, which were accompanied by pictures of the various specials.

"I should like the sweet and sour pork with vegetable rice, please," he told the youth. The other two requested the same, and the three proceeded to the cashier stop, where the server joined them on the kitchen side of the counter and rang up their bill.

When the three men had carried their generous portions of food to a table and sat down across from each other, they began rapidly shoveling in the rice, meat, and vegetables. At first their silence declared their hunger, but after a few moments one of the two younger men made a statement in his foreign tongue, which, so it appeared to the three secretaries, was abruptly contradicted by the short older man. The one who'd spoken first glanced at his contemporary, who loudly joined the discussion.

Of course, one of the women would say later to her friends, she could have been wrong, but to all of them, the direction of the conversation seemed clear, even if in a language they couldn't understand. The two younger men shouted about something they agreed on, and the older man appeared to refuse them. It was the two strong young ones against the fatter, older man— but he was firm. He spoke slowly and said little, and gradually the younger men subsided, flushed and breathing fast.

The three women quietly rose and headed for the parking lot behind the restaurant. Could they have understood the

Shona language, they would have been gratified at hearing their intuition borne out in the following dialogue: "This Tapiwa acts very incorrectly. What is he doing with this woman who is not Zimbabwean and not his wife? His time should be spent on his studies. Just because he is the son of a chief, he thinks he can do as he pleases!"

"He has never missed a class—we know this. You are jealous of this man!"

"Sir, we want to make a suggestion. What if we were to snatch his son, take him back to Zimbabwe, and let Tapiwa know he must keep his nose to the grindstone, that he is only in America to help his country and because our government has been kind enough to let him go?"

"What wild scheme is this? Always you want to stir up trouble! You know we are here for one purpose only, to check on Tapiwa and make sure he follows his instructions. He *is* following them. How could he continue his studies if he were anxious about his son?"

"Sir, the chief's grandson could be of value at home. He would be treated kindly, somewhere up country perhaps, until his father returns. We think it not such a wild scheme, sir."

"You are disappointed that our mission is almost accomplished and that we return home next week, while Tapiwa remains."

"But sir, the boy—"

"Silence! Finish your meals and remember the respect due your elder. No more wicked talk of kidnapping the boy."

37

Tapiwa was waiting at the bus stop that Wednesday morning when Chipo returned from taking Farai to PCDC. He approached her as she descended from the long, wheezing vehicle, but she walked past him, her face closed.

"Chipo, *ndapota*. Talk to me."

She walked swiftly east on New York Avenue, a fairly busy street, in the direction of the student housing units a few blocks away. Parallel to the sidewalk ran a long low wall, and behind it stood one of the mansions built by affluent East-Coast families in the late 1800s so they could winter in this area. This one looked well maintained. In front and to the side of it, spoiling its symmetry, stood a rambling ranch-style home.

She looked thinner, he thought, and her decisive stride frightened him. His heart yearned toward her; it moved him that she could be so proud with him when they both knew that right now she had no means of support beyond the meager subsistence cash he gave her from his scholarship stipend.

He moved faster, beside her, ahead of her. Then he played the only card he knew might reach her: "It's about Farai. I need to talk to you about our son."

Wearily and with no word, she sank onto the wall on their right and waited for him to speak.

"When I pick him up at the center and bring him home to you, I see he's different. He hardly speaks to me, only barely answers me if I ask him something." Tapiwa paused and gathered courage to say the hardest thing for him. His words tumbled out: "What I did is wrong, and I am sorry. I am ready to leave the girl and return to you, if you'll have me. You have been a good wife to me and I still want to be your husband."

Chipo looked at him dully.

"Would you think about it?" he pressed, and he sat down next to her—but not too close.

"I hate you for what you've done to our son, done to me," she spat. "You ruined our world. Nothing will ever be the same again for us. I curse the day I met you."

She stood suddenly as if to resume striding, and he too rose to his feet, his head bowed, waiting to hear more. She appeared to be thinking. Between them he felt an infinitely fragile wall of iridescent glass that would shatter and permanently sever their tie if he spoke.

"Perhaps," she finally began, "perhaps we could go on together, be a family again. But there is only one way for that to happen."

A passing truck drowned out her words. He gave her a blank look, so she repeated what she had said.

He wiped the sweat from his forehead and whispered, "And what way is it that you speak of?" His body braced for her reply, hoping against hope.

"We must stay in this country, Tapiwa, and not return to our native land. There is no hope for us there, only violence. We were born and grew up there, and we love that land, but we cannot return to it."

He stood quiet, silencing the words boiling up in him about his commitment, the legal impossibility of her request. Instead he asked her, "How do you suggest we do this?"

"I talked with Hannah last week. She will talk with Alexis about our circumstances. You are important to PTI, and Alexis will do all she can to help. She and Hannah are strong and knowledgeable women—they will find us a way. Especially when I tell Hannah that we may become a family again."

Her faith in a possible way to stay touched him. He remembered that Alexis had helped them when they'd arrived in September; she appeared to have no end of resources at her fingertips. Maybe Chipo had something here. She'd had some good ideas in the past. He wanted to spill out to her the story of the frightening phone call last month; she would listen, put it in perspective, share the worry. But she'd only opened the glass wall between them a tiny crack, and he knew he couldn't share his anxieties now. Better to do the most important thing first.

"If you will allow it," he told her, "when I bring Farai home tonight I will stay. I have already told the girl it's over. I will go to her apartment now and get my things."

She gave him a cold stare. "Bring him and stay, then," she told him, "but expect nothing of me. Do you understand?"

He wanted to hug her hard, hold her close, but he knew better and simply nodded. "Expect me around seven o'clock," he told her.

She reached out her right hand to him then, her left hand on her right elbow. He took it and held it as long as he dared. "Until tonight," he said.

"Until tonight." She turned and continued to walk east.

38

Wednesday afternoon

The three men in dashikis arrived in the early afternoon at Chipo Moyo's housing unit shortly after she returned. The older man had driven there in a tiny Plymouth rental; the other two held maps of Pasadena and directed his route. This time they didn't look delighted and ready to laugh. Their mien was deadly serious, their walk toward Chipo's unit purposeful. They were united in their mission—or so they appeared to Chipo.

"They wanted Tapiwa and they wanted him right then," she told Hannah an hour or so later. "Terror struck me when I saw them through my window, three strong men striding like one man. I went outside and locked the door behind me so neighbors could see us.

"How scary to be afraid of people from your own country!" Hannah said. "How did you get rid of them?"

"I just told them over and over that Tapiwa wasn't home and I did not know where he might be, and I had to catch my bus. If we had been indoors I do not know what they would have done.

They might have beaten me to get me to talk. I started to walk fast to the bus stop. People were waiting there, thank God."

It often happened that parents dropped by Hannah's office to talk, and she was grateful that Gina had left early, which created the extremely rare privacy for this conversation. Chipo had confided in her a week ago that she had considered suicide but rejected it, knowing that Farai needed her. Hannah set her message machine to automatic answer and leaned toward the young woman.

"Chipo, I haven't wanted to pry into your affairs since you told me last week that Tapiwa walked out on you and Farai and went to live with Elaine Sark. But these men harassing you and seeking him are really worrisome. Do you have time to tell me what you think about it? I'd really like to help if I could. Someone on campus could possibly assist us with this."

Chipo closed her eyes and bent her head for a quiet moment. Considering Hannah's question, she put aside her hurt and fear and visibly called on her inner strength before answering.

"You know, in our country, Hannah, Tapiwa is what you here call a prince. His father was chief of many hectares, and the chief's word decided the law; the villagers loved, respected, even feared their chief—though that didn't make his son Tapiwa wealthy when he left the village to get his education."

"So why do you think Tapiwa feels so insecure here in Pasadena?"

"Well, first, he's constantly worrying that maybe our country will withdraw his fellowship. For the rest, I'll try to tell you, but it is so complicated! Things happened so fast. You have to go back in time. You know, Zimbabwe used to be called Rhodesia, do you remember that?"

Hannah visualized the map that used to be always in view in her grade school classroom, the map with "Rhodesia" on the right side of middle Africa. Africa hadn't been on the standard curriculum at all when she attended high school, or college either.

"First we had Ian Smith's dictatorship in the seventies. In my sixth year my dad died after four years in one of Smith's prisons. For no reason at all. Some of his thugs just came to our home and took him. *Aiwa!*" Chipo's calm gave way; her voice rose. Tears coursed down her cheeks and she twisted her hands as she pictured the last time she had seen her father, twenty-six years ago when she'd been not quite three.

"Then Robert Mugabe took over, in nineteen eighty. At first, with independence, we had plenty to eat, and Zimbabwe seemed on the road to prosperity as well as democracy." She shuddered and sighed.

"I was only fourteen when Mugabe came, but I could feel the difference right away."

"Such as?" Hannah saw Chipo's half-smile as she looked back in time.

"Well, the old ways began to change. Chiefs lost their power because a lot of people moved to the cities. Women demanded rights. It made me so happy when I got to go to the University of Zimbabwe in Harare. Women at the university, un*heard* of!" she laughed. "A lot of what happened needed to happen, but it happened way too fast!"

"So, that all sounds good. Are things still going pretty well in Zimbabwe, then?"

Chipo looked at her, dumbfounded. "Hannah, do you never read the papers or watch TV? Mugabe has not been able to handle governing Zimbabwe, *at all*. It has been a disaster."

Hannah was silent, abashed by her own ignorance. Then she ventured, "Tell me about the good years, Chipo, when you were at the university."

"Well, I got my BA in nineteen eighty-eight, and my professors even encouraged me to go on for a PhD."

"Honestly? I had no idea you had opportunities like that for women in Zimbabwe."

"For a few short years we did. I got the degree in nineteen ninety-two. In sociology. Wonderful! And I met Tapiwa at the university, an engineering student. Such a happy time! But—"

"But?"

"Well, farms failed. Food got short. No gas either. Roads—you could not get from here to there anymore. Mugabe sent his troops to the Congo, so we had no law enforcement at home. Today many people starve." Chipo got up and began to pace back and forth in the office.

"You've given me a whole piece of history I knew nothing about," Hannah said thoughtfully. "You make it so clear. I'm sure you're right—too much happened too fast."

"Yes, the same thing happened in a lot of African countries." Chipo kept pacing. "At the university, I learned how long it's taken for Afro-Americans in United States to begin to have equal rights—over three hundred years. Democracy, equal rights, those changes don't happen overnight.

"But it is Tapiwa I'm sad for, son of a chief, fighting now just to survive here at PTI." She became silent.

"I am furious with him too, of course; I hate him for what he has done to us." She felt too fragile to share her recent encounter with Tapiwa and said no more about her feelings for her husband, but asked instead: "Now do you see why he is so out of his mind?"

Hannah looked up briefly and glanced to one side as the corner of her mouth tightened. She gave a wry nod, then asked, "Can you tell me anything more about why those men might be after Tapiwa?"

"Hannah, you have to understand what happened. It's like this, see—in Zimbabwe we have Shonas, they're about eighty percent of the people, and Ndebeles, about twenty percent. At first, Mugabe's Shona government didn't discriminate. But then they started to kill Ndebeles. My father, he was Ndebele; he was killed even before Mugabe came in. So that is one big thing against Tapiwa right now—his Ndebele father-in-law.

"Mugabe started the idea of our being a country, with a

flag of our own—we did not have one before him. Then he had Korean troops train his troops, and they killed most of the Ndebeles."

Chipo gave Hannah a distracted look. "Do not ask me why governments do these things. I think it is to keep the men busy, so they feel they are part of something important." She nodded her head, eyes closed, mouth in a straight line. Hannah nodded too.

"So Tapiwa, well naturally he and a lot of his friends, they want to improve things in Zimbabwe. They want to get Mugabe's ZANU party out of power. We have elections, but they are rigged so Mugabe always wins. Tapiwa jumped at the chance to come to America. He thought maybe he could get help.

"He e-mails his friends at home a lot, using a code. By the way, Mugabe did not even permit e-mail until year before last! He's paranoid, all right. But he's right to be paranoid too. A lot of people want him out, want him dead. And some in Mugabe's party suspect Tapiwa. They want him out of the way—they want to kill him." She sat again, erect on the edge of her chair.

"So that could be why those men this afternoon ..." Hannah considered.

Chipo's eyes widened as her head bobbed forward, her mouth tight. Too courteous to say, "You've finally gotten it! It's about time!" she continued, "Yes. They could know about Tapiwa's activities and want to end his life." She stood and walked to the computer, laid her hand on it unseeingly, and tapped her fingers on its grimy surface.

"I called Elaine's from downstairs, before I came up to your office, to warn him. For once he answered the phone and I did not have to deal with that horrible woman. Tapiwa said he knew the men were here in Pasadena and he would be meeting with them this afternoon. I should not worry, he would be okay, and he would bring Farai to me this evening."

"Would you be willing for me to talk with Alexis again, about these men searching for Tapiwa?"

"Alexis Storn? In the Foreign Students' Office, you mean? She helped us a lot in September. I trust her, Hannah, as I trust you. You can tell her what I have told you."

"I'm concerned for your safety, Chipo, and Tapiwa's and Farai's too. If Alexis can see us now, would you come with me to her office?"

"I feel safe here, Hannah. I'd rather you'd go, then I can do some errands and be home again when Tapiwa brings Farai home."

Hannah understood why Chipo didn't just take Farai home herself; after the threat of the visit earlier that afternoon, she needed some quiet time to recover. She asked for and received a promise from Chipo to call any time she might need help, Hannah bid her good-bye and called Alexis.

Her thoughts were dark as she waited for Alexis to pick up her phone. What Chipo had described about Zimbabwe evoked some of her own experience of Pasadena and the Los Angeles area. Unrest. Confusion. Poverty, even hunger. Shifting values. The armed holdup at Eddie's grocery. The murder, a year earlier, of the spouse of a center staff member.

Pasadena Technological Institute, with its successful professors and programs and its beautifully manicured campus and surrounding attractive residential area, appeared at this moment like the mirage of a lush oasis. It seemed as if no one there saw what she saw.

39

"Alexis, could you see me if I come over now? It's urgent."

Hannah enjoyed an ongoing relationship with Alexis. She frequently received calls from her to enter children on the center's long wait list, children from Norway, Taiwan, Australia, France, Spain, India. One of Hannah's joys was the early intermingling and friendships formed between children and families from different cultures, something that would be part of who they were for all their lives. The center couldn't always offer an immediate space, but Alexis planned well and usually called months before the child and family's expected arrival.

"Sure, Hannah, come on over. I'm just putting the office to bed for the night," Alexis' husky voice assured her.

Hannah put on her walking shoes, ducked downstairs, and told Anne in the fours room where she might be reached and that she expected to be back by five thirty, half an hour before closing time. Then she walked briskly south on campus, away from the mountains and toward Alexis' building. Students zoomed by on their bikes like bats in the dusk. Pedestrians needed to keep their ears attuned for the sudden whir of their tires and be certain not to move to the left or falter in their course. Several accidents involving pedestrians and bikers had recently taken place, though none that she knew of had resulted in more than minor injuries.

Hannah loved the way the walk stretched her calves and loosened her back muscles. Faculty and students—those who didn't remain for research or lab experiments in the evening— hurried through the chill air from offices to cars or dorms. No abundant flowers bloomed on the campus at this time of year, but fruit and silk floss trees were beginning to bud and whole beds of agapanthus sported tall stalks bulging with what soon would be pale purple blossoms. Hannah pulled open the heavy wooden door of the old Public Affairs building and turned left down the hall toward Foreign Student Aid.

"How lucky for me that you're free!" she greeted Alexis, who was seated at her desk. Alexis' clutter-free office welcomed her with its soft chairs, thriving plants, and paintings on the walls—paintings that Alexis changed from time to time. In her free hours she both drew and painted very creditably, Hannah knew. Alexis had studied painting in Paris in the sixties. Hannah had lived there with her professor husband and family during the same years, neither woman aware of the other's existence then. Now, the experience bonded them. Alexis' auburn hair, pleasant face, intelligent eyes, and comfortably limber figure fit Hannah's idea of a capable administrator. Hannah found her down-to-earth, discreet, and knowledgeable.

"So Hannah, what's up?"

"Have you heard anything about three African men on campus today? I heard from Chipo Moyo—remember I talked with you about finding a job for her last week—"

Alexis snapped her fingers in a *Zut!* gesture, and pursed her lips. "Oh, of course! It's I who should have called you, but for the moment I'd forgotten about that center connection of Tapiwa's.

"But to answer your question, yes, we know about the men.

Sometimes the two younger ones are seen alone, and sometimes they're with an older man. Campus security isn't sure whether they're directly from Zimbabwe or are ex-pats who've lived in the Los Angeles area awhile. We're concerned about their intentions for Tapiwa, and—this is confidential of course—we've alerted the sheriff's department about it. I don't know whether the sheriff plans to put Elaine Sark's apartment under surveillance, but we think it might be a good idea."

Hannah exhaled. "Does Kevin Drabb know about this?"

"Yes. It was he who decided to call in the sheriff, because the campus police don't carry weapons and don't have the authority to offer protection in a case like this."

Hannah looked relieved. "I know how Kevin hates to bring in county services on campus matters. But I'm glad he did this time. Those men went to Tapiwa's wife today and put a lot of pressure on her. She's strong, though, and refused to give them information. She told me she'd called Tapiwa and warned him."

Alexis nodded. "Kevin's office warned Tapiwa too, but he shook off what they told him, said he could handle anything that might come up."

"I guess that matter's in good hands, and we can only hope nothing ugly happens," Hannah opined.

"My other question for you—and I know we already talked about this last week—is can't we find some way that Chipo, Tapiwa's wife, can earn some cash? Besides cleaning houses, I mean.

"She's had some real lows this fall—actually considered taking her own life at one point, she told me, but realized she could never do it with her little son to think about. As you know, she's a sociology PhD and has many skills. She worked in the census bureau in Harare collecting data, at quite a high level, I think. She'd do almost any kind of work here, and my opinion is that Tapiwa's manhood would be greatly assuaged if more money were in the family bank account." Hannah felt a little tired from delivering so much information.

"He doesn't mind her being the breadwinner?"

"Apparently not," Hannah responded. "His scholarship brings in a small monthly stipend, so it's not as if he brings in nothing. In Harare she supported the family while he finished his engineering degree. I think he'd be delighted if she could help out now. I know you know every rule and loophole about working while on a visa, and I hope you can figure something out." She let her eyes rest on a new painting of what appeared to be a seagull attempting a landing in stormy weather.

"I have an idea on that, Hannah, and I promise you I'll work on it. Tapiwa's here on a J-1 visa, sponsored by the Zimbabwean and the United States governments. He and Chipo are still legally married, so as his dependent wife, she can apply to the United States Immigration for permission to work. A lot of dependent spouses apply for it, and permission's usually granted." Alexis' gaze followed Hannah's to the painting.

"That's so good to hear! My intuition about Tapiwa is that he's still stunned by culture shock and considers himself still married, just taking a break. He assumes he and Chipo will get together again."

Alexis rolled her eyes. "Right. I know that's crazy, but I see this kind of thing from time to time, and I know you're right— often the husband's attitudes are just what you described."

"He's very unrealistic about what she's going through. If the financial picture improved, one of his big anxieties would go away, and he could focus more on his studies. Chipo could probably even help him with some of his assignments. Engineering's not her field, but she's a bright woman," Hannah continued.

Alexis nodded. "You're right, her skills are wasted right now, and they could be put to good use. And yes, it might even get him out of Elaine Sark's clutches! I don't mean this as gossip, but Elaine's known as the campus Monica Lewinsky. Her last live-in was single, but she usually goes after married men. It's a mess, and Elaine and Tapiwa should straighten up and go their separate ways, is my opinion!"

Both women knew their opinions counted for absolutely nothing in the lives of the people they spoke about, but it eased them to talk in confidence about them. Hannah felt relieved to know that the International Students' Office, the campus police, and the sheriff already knew of Tapiwa's possible danger. Especially the sheriff. And all this without need for her to convince Kevin that the sheriff's office should be alerted. Almost too good to believe.

"I feel so much better now that I've talked with you. How come that's often the case?" she joked to Alexis as she prepared to walk back to the center for closing time. Sometimes, she mused, the gods did smile on her life.

"*Au revoir, mon ami,*" and with a wave, Hannah left her friend. She loved this time of the day at the center. Though the staff would be tired now and the winter's early dark would intensify the children's need for their parents, she knew she'd feel pleasure and renewal just being with them. She hurried back across campus as the shadows gathered.

40

This center is my home base, Hannah thought, *my touchstone.*
She sat on the rug and read *The Tenth Good Thing About Barney* to a small group of children. Hannah loved Judith Viorst's wise and comforting story about Barney, a recently-deceased cat, and its young owner.

"My sister's dog died last year," volunteered Su-ling.

"I have a kitten, but she's not grown yet," Anan said.

"It's sad when you lose your pet," Adam summed it up.

Definitely the right book to read a few days after the rabbit's mysterious death, which seemed to Hannah symptomatic of the random violence at post offices, in school yards, and in hot spots around the world. She hoped deeply that by working along with parents to help children find and learn peaceful ways of relating to each other, she and the staff—and thousands of parents, other child care centers, and family day care homes—might make a difference, might tip the balance toward sanity and peace in the world. Cynics might scoff, but Hannah believed it could happen.

The warm, brightly lit fours room had a surreal quality, and the deep darkness and cold just outside seemed to press through windows and doors. Parents hurried in, their faces softening and brightening at the sight of their children. At six o'clock the late-fee system began. It charged parents an increasing amount for every five minutes late, or part thereof. Parents who were held up by work or traffic found it hard to make the deadline.

It was six past six, and three children were still unclaimed. Their responses varied: Anan, a much-loved child, appeared oblivious; Adam philosophically began to assemble a puzzle; Farai alone could not hide his anxiety and sat with his jacket already on, scanning the doorway where his father should appear. Anan's mother and Adam's nanny picked up their charges. Farai rocked back and forth, humming nonstop.

Tapiwa Moyo walked through the door, and Farai jumped up and threw his arms around him, almost unbalancing the tall young man. Tapiwa hugged his son back, spoke to him in Shona, then turned to Hannah, "He's glad to see me, isn't it?" His occasional idioms, odd to her ear, were endearing as well.

"He painted a picture of you this morning, Tapiwa," Hannah responded, wishing she knew how to bridge the culture barrier and tell him about how this boy looked up to his father and acted out at school some of the hurt and confusion he felt right now. She hated to give Tapiwa a late slip that would appear later on his tuition invoice, but fairness decreed that each of the late parents be given their slips. She watched the young father and his small son leave the room, and mentally enveloped them in love. These caring waves she felt and sent out were almost an unconscious thing. If you'd asked her, she could only have told you that in some sense these young families who entrusted their children to her center were her responsibility.

Anne had taken care of the end-of-the-day tasks—she'd pulled shades, set up the sign-in sheet for the next day, replaced the last LEGO sets, puzzles, and play props, and set the small chairs on the low tables for the early-morning cleaners. She shrugged into her jacket.

"Good night, Hannah, see you tomorrow." She left, locking the door behind her.

Tomorrow would be the weekly Thursday staff meeting, and the agenda for it had to be in all staff members' boxes by morning, so Hannah climbed the stairs to her office and began to compose.

It was more fun creating the staff agenda than writing a board report, because throughout the week teachers talked to Hannah about subjects they wanted discussed and she'd scribble them down and drop them into the agenda folder. An easy job, then, to organize these into related groups, arrange them in order of importance, and assemble the finished product. She felt glad, too, that Ben had been able to fix the printer—she'd had it back since Friday afternoon and it printed smoothly again.

Sirens sounded faintly a few blocks away, and in one part of her mind she unconsciously visualized the rain extinguishing a fire. She looked in her cartoon file and found one that was relevant for her agenda—Dilbert poking fun at management—and taped it at the bottom, hoping to warm up the document with a note of humor. Maybe staff might get the message that she could see their point of view as well as "management's." It still puzzled her to be regarded as "the boss." She'd come up herself from mixing paints and hauling tricycles, the lowest possible position at a preschool, and still thought of herself as simply one of the teaching team, the one responsible for facilitating the teachers' work.

She walked from one building to another, dropping an agenda in each staff member's mailbox. It was seven o'clock when she finished.

Bone-tired but satisfied, she felt ready to go home.

41

Na Li pizza stand near PCDC
Wednesday, January 20, 1999

Holding his young son's hand was what kept him going these days, Tapiwa thought. He stood with Farai in the dusk just outside the circle of light cast by the pizza stand generator, waiting to order a slice of pizza. He'd have liked one for himself too—the rich red-and-yellow sight of it in the brightly lit stand, the smells of garlic and cheese, even the sounds of the dough being slapped into a round and the toaster oven slammed into place by the little man in the stand spoke loud to his empty stomach.

But with money so tight, when it was his turn to order he would ask for one piece only, chicken garlic, Farai's favorite. Anyway, he knew Farai would honor his father by offering him the first bite. That was their way, their way that went back through time.

While they waited in the growing darkness, Tapiwa looked around at the others. Mostly they were young parents like him, accompanied by one or two children just picked up from PCDC.

An old Ford idled at the curb, with two figures inside, their heads turned toward him—he could see that much from the light cast by the pizza stand. Next to him stood Aaron's mother Sue, alone. The few other adults he recognized from the center he knew not by name, but only as the parent of a child in Farai's group. Sue seemed unsteady on her feet. *Where was her husband?* Then he remembered: it was only in the old days, the days of his parents and grandparents, that husbands and wives took care of each other. Today just taking care of yourself took all your energy and time.

He handed his wallet to Farai for a moment as he moved forward to order. Then he heard an urgent shout—"Look out!"—and in the glimpse of a split second, saw a cyclist skid toward the stand, which was parked on gravel.

Pop! Darkness suddenly blotted out the pizza stand lights. Tapiwa heard a horrible, out-of-control, sliding *gretttttch,* a metallic clang, and the low tinkle of splintered glass as it hit the sidewalk. The dark wheeled form that had hurtled into the stand ricocheted backward into the group, and Farai stood directly in its path. Paralyzed, Tapiwa saw these events in terrible slow motion.

Wait. In a dream just after Farai's birth he'd seen his son endangered, and he remembered from the dream what he had to do. With all his strength he lurched close to his son, shoved him out of the bicyclist's trajectory, and took its full force against his own belly and chest. He fell so hard that onlookers later said his head pounded more than once on the cold concrete—though in the dark they couldn't really have seen this. Maybe they just remembered the sound.

A few minutes later sheriff cars and rescue van from the nearby fire station roared to the scene. Sirens screamed and blared and lights blinded the paramedics as they searched for victims. They found Tapiwa's body. Blood oozed from his mouth and ears, fluid leaked from the back of his head, his eyes rolled back into their sockets. They saw his contorted neck, his head at a horrible angle. The officer in charge searched Tapiwa's pockets. He found no identification.

A woman's scream stabbed their ears. "Farai! Farai! Where are you?"

The bicyclist was doubled up next to a small, bare camphor tree, banging his head against it, groaning, "Oh my God. Is he all right?" A fireman squatted next to him, his arm firm around the man's shoulders. The parents with children had scurried quickly toward the warmth of their homes, thankful to be alive, their children's vulnerability hitting them as hard as the out-of-control cyclist, moments earlier, had hit Tapiwa.

Tapiwa felt his father's spirit take his hand. He and the old chief strolled through the long veldt grasses together, holding their staffs, just the two of them. He heard a heron's call, smelled the aloe blossoms. How good it felt to be home at last.

42

It was seven o'clock, and Hannah was finally free to head home. Though she lived only a mile away, she often drove rather than walked at this time of year. As had happened this evening, her work frequently kept her until well after dark, and she was tired and hungry. She double-checked that all entrances to the center were securely locked and headed out into the night. From a distance came shouts and the throb of heavy motors. She slumped into her Camry and drove the short distance home.

The modest Spanish-style bungalow reached out, as always, to welcome her. She entered, lit the gas pipe in the fireplace, and set three logs over it as her husband had taught her long ago. Sweetpea greeted her warmly with a purred ankle rub as Hannah surveyed an array of deli entrees in her freezer compartment.

Egg rolls tonight? Or chicken enchilada?

While the microwave warmed the enchilada, she made a quick tossed salad and poured a glass of red wine.

"I never drink alone," a friend had told her in somber tones at the time of her husband's death ten years earlier, but Hannah found her nightly glass a comfort. She faced the fire while reading her mail, ate dinner, then cleared up, attended to phone messages, and fell into bed with her current book, a biography of Ernest Hemingway.

My time, just for me.

Friends knew not to call after nine. Most of the books she read were recommended by a friend or had been recently reviewed in the Sunday *New York Times*. Occasionally she read something she'd heard about over the last forty years but never had time to read—a pocket of history like the Dreyfus affair or Genghis Kahn, or a novel by Henry James or Willa Cather. Her reading connected her to her past—growing up as the child of a literature professor, and her marriage to Jim, a historian. For fifteen or twenty minutes before sleep seized her, Hannah gratefully lost herself in worlds far removed.

❦   ❦   ❦

Brutally shrill, the phone woke her only an hour later, at eleven ten p.m.

"Hannah, Farai's gone missing!" Chipo's near-incoherent voice sliced through the remnants of Hannah's slumber. "His dad said he'd bring him to me after the center closed tonight, but he never came. I called that slut Elaine—"

"Oh Chipo! Was Farai there?"

"*Aiwa*, Hannah, no! I'm calling you because he's gone missing!" Even in her desperation, Chipo tried to be clear.

"She told me, 'Bitch, you'll never see him again!' Did you see Tapiwa this evening when he picked up Farai? Did he say anything unusual? Have you any idea where he went?"

Her voice gave way to sobs, and Hannah used the moment to clear her head and think. She moved around her now-frigid room, closed the window, and, shivering, flicked on the wall heater, grateful for her cordless phone.

"Chipo, I'm so sorry. I want to help. I didn't notice anything different about Tapiwa when he picked up Farai, but you know better than anyone how weird he's been since last month. Have you called the sheriff's office?"

Chipo broke again into sobs, then suddenly stopped herself. "I shall never in my life call the sheriff, Hannah."

Hannah understood. "Do you want me to come over?" She wouldn't have made this offer if Chipo weren't alone in Pasadena, with no family except her now-absent husband and little son, and as yet no real friends. Hannah knew, too, that the culture shock had been almost unbearable, not to mention the difficulty of living on Tapiwa's meager student stipend.

In fact, the only steady factor in Chipo's life here had been Farai's full-time attendance at PCDC. His child care subsidy, Chipo had told Hannah, was a holdover from the heady days of Mugabe's early eighties takeover of Zimbabwe, when students were sent abroad to study and return to build the country. Now, with Zimbabwe in turmoil, Chipo lived in fear that the child care part of Tapiwa's scholarship might be terminated at any time.

What could Tapiwa be thinking of, dumping his wife and now spiriting away their son?

"I'll be there, Chipo, as soon as I can. Are you at the place on North Roosevelt?" Hannah riffled through her center directory.

"Same place, Hannah. Please hurry." Chipo hung up.

What can I possibly do to help, besides be with her?

She rang Kevin Drabb's number. No answer. "Kevin," she told his answer machine, "it's eleven twenty. Chipo Moyo just called me. She expected Tapiwa Moyo to bring their son to her this evening. He didn't, and he hasn't called her. I'm going to her home now. Here's the number of the pay phone outside Chipo's housing unit."

She snatched up two tea bags and headed for her car. Responding to this kind of crisis didn't appear in her job description, but situations this serious were now happening with what seemed increased frequency.

She drove east along Del Monte toward Chipo's housing unit, braked suddenly at the Allen Avenue signal, and turned north. Her heart ached as she turned right on New York Drive toward the seedy units where Chipo lived. She turned right again, down Roosevelt, and noted the trash overflowing the dumpster for Chipo's section: a dispiriting mass of disposable diapers, bottles, and food-stained Styrofoam containers. Hannah tried to imagine how these Pasadena housing units appeared to Chipo, and even more, what might be the effects of such sights on young children everywhere, like Farai receiving their first impressions of our planet.

43

Chipo stood at the gate to the housing project, disheveled and wild-eyed and waving her arms, dressed in the same white flowered top and blue jeans she'd worn that afternoon. Hannah spotted the white windmill and braked.

"Hannah! I thought you'd never get here!"

Hannah leaned over and opened the passenger door. Before she could speak, Chipo froze.

"Do you hear the phone?"

Hannah listened. "No, I hear nothing, Chipo."

"I've listened so hard for that phone. I was sure I heard it."

Both women listened intently, but they heard nothing, so Chipo got in the car and they drove to the other end of the apartment complex, parking near Chipo's unit. When they got out of the car Hannah gave Chipo a long, close hug, then followed her inside and, without asking, headed to the stove, filled a pan with water, turned on the gas, and began looking for mugs.

"Chipo, are you sure Farai's still with Tapiwa?"

"Of course not! I'm not sure of anything! But I think so, because Tapiwa takes good care of his son, Hannah, even though he treats *me* like dirt! Oh God, he used to be so loving to me, but since we came here he's completely changed." She rocked forward and back, moaning softly. Even as her heart melted for Chipo, Hannah was shocked to witness such grief in a woman usually so proud, self-sufficient, and strong.

She rinsed two chipped mugs under the ancient faucet and threw in the Sleepytime tea bags she'd brought.

We probably need coffee here for thinking, but maybe soothing tea's better.

"You're right—Tapiwa's a loving dad. And he did pick up Farai just after closing time this evening."

Hannah paused as her eyes met Chipo's. "Chipo, we *must* call the sheriff now. Your son's life may be in danger."

"He would be in greater danger in the sheriff's clutches! Hannah, I will not let you make that phone call. I will not! Police, sheriffs, they are *evil!*" Chipo rushed to her front door, blocked it, and glared at Hannah, who stared at her open-mouthed, taken aback at Chipo's rigid body and bulging eyes.

Chipo hurled each word at Hannah. "The sheriff is *not—to—be—called.*"

"Chipo," she asked, "this sheriff thing. Is it because of what you told me this afternoon? Because of your dad?"

"I shall never call the sheriff, Hannah. I think you understand," Chipo stated, straightening and finding her dignity once more.

"I'll wait until morning, then, Chipo," Hannah told her, "but I do plan to try again to reach Kevin Drabb on campus, on your pay phone, and our board president, Andrew, needs to know about this as well."

With as steady a step as she could muster, Hannah squeezed past Chipo and went to the pay phone. She had change in her pocket and knew the numbers by heart. She made another unsuccessful call to Kevin. Then she punched in Andrew's number, awakening him. She informed him of Farai's disappearance and Chipo's refusal to call the sheriff.

"So you're with her, Hannah? And we don't know where Tapiwa is? But he left the Center with Farai just after six?"

"Yes, yes, and yes, Andrew. Can you please call the sheriff's office to report the missing child? Ask that Sheriff Bronson be notified, please."

"This is really scary, Hannah. Of course I'll make the call for you. Will you and Chipo be okay until morning?"

"Okay until morning. That will be my mantra for the next few hours. Thanks for understanding—thanks for being there," Hannah said, then clicked the receiver back in its niche and turned back toward Chipo.

Inside again, she went to a chair—one of only two in the room—and patted it, motioning for Chipo to sit. Then she knelt beside the terrified woman. She held her arm around Chipo for nearly an hour, until she felt the young woman's body begin to loosen and sag. In its awkward position, Hannah's own body began to ache, but gradually relaxed as Chipo's did. They shared the silence, and what had been a cold distance between them became a warm connection, shelter for them both.

"Hannah, what can we do?" Chipo finally asked.

"Let me call Elaine again and see if she'll talk to me." Chipo gave her Elaine's number, and Hannah went outside and tried again but got a busy signal. She punched O and asked for an emergency intercept but the operator told her that such an intercept wasn't possible.

Then she rang Kevin Drabb again, and again reached his phone machine, leaving a third message. Twice more during the long night she called Kevin and left the message: Farai is missing.

Re-entering Chipo's living room, she told her, "I think it best we stay where we are, my dear. Tapiwa knows you're waiting here for him and Farai. Maybe something has detained him, but I know if he's able to, he'll come."

"If we leave, he won't know where to find me," Chipo agreed. "Oh Hannah, I'm hurting so much!"

Chipo sat, almost fell, on Farai's bed, and ran her hand over and over the nightshirt and slippers she'd laid out for him. She stared at the wall through bloodshot eyes. "I used to believe nothing worse could happen when my father died in prison. Then when Tapiwa left me for that slut, I thought nothing worse than that could happen. Tonight, with Farai missing, I *know* nothing worse could ever, ever happen." Chipo's rhythmic words sounded like an ancient chant.

Hannah noted the tiny mug sitting on the table, the carefully folded napkin, the child-sized fork and spoon, and the plate with Mickey Mouse smiling cheerfully at its center and alphabet letters around the rim.

The two women sustained each other through the rest of the night. Hannah dozed intermittently, but Chipo sat erect, swaying, hugging herself as she held Farai's furry slipper to her cheek, her eyes open wide, listening for the phone or a step outside.

Toward six, Hannah went to the phone, fished in her handbag for the center directory she always carried with her, and placed a call to Sekai Turino. Someone picked up the receiver and hung up. She returned to Chipo.

"May I call Sue? Maybe she could keep you company."

Chipo's rocking continued as she shook her head, "No, I will be all right."

Hannah hugged her, assured her she would stay in close touch, and left for the center.

44

Thursday morning
6:15 a.m.

Speeding toward the center, Sekai noted Joan's battered Studebaker parked outside the entrance to the infant room, three blocks from Hannah's office.

Joan's not due here yet. And why is her car here instead of by the fours room? Come to think of it, where has she been all week? I've not seen her.

Since it was early, Sekai easily found a parking space in the lot two blocks from the center and loped, almost ran, toward Hannah's office. Joan stood perfectly still in the doorway, as yet unaware of her approach. Something about her stance told Sekai more clearly than words that she was anxious. *Why?*

Sekai had never felt comfortable around Joan, who, as lead teacher, was one of her superiors. In her urgency to get to Hannah, she wished she could avoid her now, but Joan spotted her and immediately headed her way. Sekai had to face her.

"How are you, and what brings you so early this morning,

Joan?" she asked with her customary courtesy, as casually as she could.

"I could ask you the same. Don't you usually start at eight thirty?" Joan shot back. "Actually, I'm not working the rest of this week. But I want to talk with Hannah for a few minutes. That's why I'm here." In a warmer tone she asked, "Something the matter, Sekai? You look a little worried, not like your usual calm self."

Her words were kind and her tone touched fear and sadness in Sekai she hadn't realized were so strong. She allowed Joan to comfort her with a hug, then told her, "I'm on my way to find Hannah too, and ask her for some advice."

"Advice? Sekai, may I ask about what? Maybe I could help, dear. I think Hannah's pretty busy this morning, what with today's staff meeting to prepare for. Sometimes she comes in early like this just to have a little quiet work time alone."

Immediately Sekai felt the impropriety of her plan. Yes, she saw now that her visit would be an intrusion upon Hannah. At the back of her mind she was always an outsider, black and from another country, and this consciousness overtook her now. Sekai trusted Hannah, but she also knew that her boss, like Joan and many of her coworkers here at the center, was Anglo and American-born. Joan, as one of the six lead teachers, was perhaps the more proper person to take her problem to Hannah, Sekai reasoned. Maybe she should entrust her information, and her urgent question about how to proceed, to Joan. She saw that now.

"Can we talk a little somewhere nearby?" she asked.

"Maybe in your car, if that's okay with you," Joan suggested, and they headed back toward the parking lot in the direction from which Sekai had come. A golden retriever and a terrier bounded by them. Early-morning dog walkers carrying plastic bags took advantage of the spacious campus lawns and deserted pathways, letting their dogs run free on the dewy grass.

The two women got into Sekai's Ford Galaxy, and Joan

turned expectantly toward Sekai, who sat behind the steering wheel.

She could hardly find words to begin, but Joan listened receptively, and despite Sekai's misgivings, she told her the problem about which she had come to ask Hannah's advice.

"And I thought maybe I could drive up to Chipo's to let her know her mother is here, before I'm due at eight thirty at the center, but I thought Hannah should know first, and maybe she would have some good sense for me," she concluded.

Joan's face looked almost deliberately blank, and this quickened Sekai's anxiety; she concentrated on the tight buds on a pear tree and willed herself to appreciate its beauty against the morning sky. After a long moment Joan broke the silence between them. She spoke in a crisp, authoritative tone.

"I'm glad you let me know about this, Sekai. You did the right thing. I know how hard all this must be for you. Hannah's car's outside her office, so I know she's there. I'll just go and talk with her now—I'm sure she'll give me priority when I tell her what it's about—and then I'll get back to you as fast as I can. Will you be in the infant room?"

"I can wait there, I guess. It is not my shift yet, but I feel safe there, and I can find things to do while I wait." She wanted to add a plea that Joan hurry but did not think it her place to do so.

The women hurried back toward Hannah's office, and Joan turned into the small building that housed the office while Sekai walked the three blocks back to the infant room.

A flock of raucous parrots flew overhead, reminding her of days long gone by. In the infant play yard she stooped and picked up a stray wooden part for one of the bright green and red trains the babies had played with the day before. She paused at the door, said a brief prayer according to her custom, and then, at six thirty, entered the peaceful room where her small charges would soon arrive. The lead teacher of the infant group folded diapers in the next room. No babies had yet arrived.

45

The office seemed unusually quiet at this early hour. Hannah was cradling the phone to her ear. As Joan entered, she noticed immediately and with pleasure that Hannah's hair was untidy and her pants and top wrinkled. Joan smelled lavender. Hannah kept the herb oil in her desk and had once laughingly confessed to Joan that she dabbed it behind her ears to alleviate stress.

"Hannah Cooper at the center, with a message for you, Alexis. It's six thirty a.m. and I need to see you as soon as your office opens—it's urgent. I'll be over there at eight thirty. Thanks." She hung up the phone.

"Problem, Hannah?" Joan asked in a sympathetic tone.

"Yes Joan, but I'm sure it will get solved. I saw you out there with Sekai just now. What brings you here today?"

Joan opened her mouth to reply, but Hannah continued, "I'm available for a few minutes if you need me, but I came early to work on something else and I need to get to it." She tried to sound composed.

Why did she so often perceive Joan as a wily chess opponent? Chess had never been Hannah's forte. She cheerfully lost most chess matches to her grandchildren and found it difficult to remember the powers and limitations of each piece. At a leadership conference years ago someone had told her that knowledge of chess was essential to directing a business or a school.

She moved her chair from behind the desk, hoping that removing the barrier between them would indicate her readiness to listen. She also hoped that Joan hadn't come to talk about their appointment the next day, as she needed her energy now for the Chipo-Farai matter. Hannah resolved to listen very carefully to what Joan said.

"I have a pretty good idea what our appointment tomorrow's about," Joan began, "and I really want to keep my job at the center, Hannah. As you know, this place has been like home to me for a lot of years, way before you came here. I'm sorry I've been late so often recently—"

Recently! All these years, she's been late, and late, and late. Aloud she said, "Joan, surely you didn't come here so early to discuss this again?"

"You're a smart lady, Hannah, always have been."

Hannah straightened herself in her chair and visualized herself taking a complete yoga breath.

"And you're right, I didn't come this morning to discuss lateness. As a matter of fact, I have some information about one of our children that could be very important to you." Joan sat back and waited expectantly.

"Well, and what might that be?"

"I wonder how much you might want to hear it." Joan's openly menacing tone increased Hannah's shock; Joan had completely abandoned her usual soft, gentle manner of speech.

Could this possibly have to do with Farai's whereabouts? Hannah wondered. *But how would Joan even know him to be missing?* Joan wanted to bargain her knowledge, whatever it was, in return for her job. She was taking Hannah by surprise, more than twenty-four hours before her termination interview, bringing her termination into play and inserting it into the matter of—maybe—Farai's disappearance.

Hannah could feign ignorance of Joan's meaning, could thrust and parry, but beneath Joan's words the message was clear, as was the choice Joan was forcing upon her: Hannah could promise to go to the personnel committee and secure a reprieve for Joan and thereby learn something important, or she could hang tough and possibly risk someone's safety. If Joan's information turned out to be about Farai, and what Hannah had heard about his father's politics was true, the risk might even be to his life.

"Joan, I don't know what information you have or who it's about, but if it has to do with one of our center children's safety and well being, then of course I want to hear it, and I expect you to tell it to me, *now. Immediately. This minute.*" Hannah straightened in her chair, head erect, shoulders jutting; her eyes drilled into Joan's.

It was now Joan's turn to be surprised by Hannah's firm, stern tone. "Okay, can you help me keep my job? What I know may help you keep yours."

It was unconscionable, Joan threatening her like this. Should she make a false promise in order to get this information?

"I'm not one to play games, Joan—you know that. I don't know what my job has to do with anything."

"You know, Hannah, you're not the only one around here with important information. I'm not at liberty to tell you why your job might be in question," Joan spoke firmly, "but it definitely could be. And yes, a child's safety's at stake here."

Is she bluffing?

"So you essentially offer me this information under conditions?"

"Yes. My condition, as you call it, is that I remain at the center in my present job," Joan spoke insolently, her eyes glittered green. "I need you to call Andrew now while I listen on the other phone, and tell him the decision to fire me tomorrow's off. And in return, I can tell you right now the location of the child you were talking about on the phone when I came in."

It was almost seven o'clock now, and Gina's steps could be heard outside on the stairs; she usually arrived a few moments early. She would wonder about the closed door.

A soft knock, and Gina put in her head. "May I come in?"

"In a few minutes, Gina. We're just finishing a conference here. I'll open the door as soon as we're done." Hannah spoke as calmly as she could.

"Ho-kay," Gina's voice rose expressively on the second syllable as she took in the unexpected sight of her boss and one of the lead teachers in conference so early. She quickly closed the door.

"Joan, I'll do almost anything when the safety of one of our children's involved." It was true, and Joan knew it. "Get on Gina's phone, and I'll try to reach Andrew—but how do I know you're telling me the truth?"

Joan spoke slowly: "A son did not come home to his mother last night. And a daughter doesn't even know her mother has come. But," she sneered, "*I* keep track of these things. Some director you are, Hannah—you don't know half of what goes on here at 'your' Center." Her mocking laugh shrilled out.

"Are you speaking of Farai?" Hannah's words were obliterated by the thunder of heavy, fast steps on the stairs. Before Joan could speak, Deputy Sheriff Patrick Bronson strode into the small office. His annoyance was unmistakable.

"Hannah, I need to speak with you. Alone." Gone was the warm, casual Southern intonation. His piercing blue eyes swept over Joan, willing her instant departure. Joan retreated toward the stairs.

"Talk to you later, Hannah." She threw the words lightly over her shoulder.

46

In the infant room, Sekai waited for Joan and meditated. The light began to filter in through the east windows onto the cribs in the next room, the nest of pillows to her left, the low shelves filled with soft toys. A colorful poster on the opposite wall showed a seated caregiver, tenderly holding a baby on his knees, looking into the infant's eyes and offering him a blue plastic ring from a multicolored stack.

Zero to nine's the crucial time.

Then in smaller print: *Cognitive development begins and grows from relationships built on trust.*

Peaceful as the setting was, Sekai felt anxious and restless. Ruvimbo counted on her. What would come of Joan's interview with Hannah? She glanced out the window and saw Joan striding toward her car, looking furious. Sekai realized that whatever had transpired during her interview with Hannah, Joan would not tell her, Sekai, about it. She also saw a sheriff's car in front of Hannah's office.

It was almost two hours before her scheduled time to work.

Why not let Chipo know her mother was here? She must go talk to Ruvimbo.

Sekai jumped up, left the infant room, walked quickly to her car, and drove the short distance to her apartment. It felt better to be in motion—and headed away from the sheriff's car. She parked, sprinted up the stairs, and knocked softly on her apartment door, her breath quick, rasping. Ruvimbo let her in, eyes wide with wondering what Sekai had to tell her.

"Dear friend, I still have no news," Sekai whispered. "I saw a sheriff's car parked in front of Hannah's office, so I've come back to you without talking first with her."

Ruvimbo's face fell. "And what of Chipo, then?" she asked.

"I, too, am thinking of Chipo," Sekai answered, "and I think we must tell her right away that you are here."

"Can we phone her?"

"I'm scared that the phone where she lives may be tapped, Ruvimbo."

"Could you drive there, then?" Ruvimbo quavered.

"Always our thoughts go along the same path!" Sekai patted her friend's arm. "I will go to Chipo now, before work. If I have time I will return to you this morning and let you know what happened."

"And if not? Will I need to wait here?" Ruvimbo looked alarmed at this prospect.

"I'm afraid so, my friend. But I will try very hard to get you word as soon as I can. With no private phone at Chipo's, it will be difficult. And you may have to wait until two thirty, when I get off work."

"Go immediately, then! And may your mission be successful!"

Ruvimbo hugged her friend and pushed her toward the door. Her hands were gentle, but her eyes were glazed with worry.

47

Daily Pasadena Press
Thursday, January 21, 1999

Pasadena Technological Institute Student
Killed in Bicycle Accident—Child Missing

An out-of-control cyclist ploughed into a crowd of waiting pizza customers yesterday evening, killing a Pasadena Technological Institute student and injuring two others. Tapiwa Moyo, an engineering student at PTI, died instantly when George Vincent, a local computer technician, lost control of his bicycle. Moyo's son, four-year-old Farai Moyo, disappeared in the aftermath of the accident. A thorough search of the area has been made, and all leads are being pursued, Los Angeles County Sheriff's Department spokesperson Wendell Holmes said.

Vincent told sheriff personnel that a generator failure at the Na-Li pizza stand on Del Vista Avenue and Fill Street distracted him around 6:30 p.m. He said the sudden loud noise and subsequent abrupt darkness caused him to jam on his brakes and skid into the crowd.

Sheila Abrams and Marcel Pinot, also PTI students, were slightly injured and released at the scene of the accident.

"We heard a loud crack, there was a blackout and then screams as this bicycle crashed into people at the pizza stand. Moyo's head hit the concrete so hard that apparently it cracked his skull," said witness Marjorie Simpson.

The Sheriff's Department is investigating the incident. Vincent is under arrest but will likely be released after his arraignment today, Holmes said.

Holmes requests that anyone with information or a lead about the child's disappearance call his office, day or night.

48

"Hannah, what's this all about? Why didn't you call us when Ms. Moyo called you last night?" Deputy Sheriff Bronson shouted over his walkie talkie's harsh static buzz. Always a cordial colleague in the past, he now stood stiff and grim just inside her closed office door. His muscular body was encased in official gear, complete with badge and insignia, baton, and holstered gun. His blue gaze beneath the thick gray regulation haircut was steely.

She cocked her head. "How did you know that Chipo called me?"

"Not because *you* told me, that's for sure. Hannah, *I'm* the one to ask questions here. So, why didn't you call me when Ms. Moyo called you last night?"

"The reasons why I didn't call your office last night are exactly what we talked about last week, about campus policy toward our center, Sheriff." As she spoke, both her head and her voice rose and fell slightly, and her eyes widened for emphasis.

"Did Drabb tell you to call him in the middle of the night if necessary?"

"Yes, actually, he did. But I can't always reach him. I did

call him more than once last night even though Chipo begged me not to. I did call Andrew Chin, our board president, and he said he'd call your office—"

"Hannah, in a possible kidnap case you know you should have called me when you couldn't reach Drabb." His tone sounded as if he addressed a very young child, his lips pursed and his stare intense.

"Sheriff, from the moment Chipo's call woke me, my one thought was to get to her. I heard her desperation and I knew, too, that she's been very emotionally unstable since her husband left her. She'd even considered suicide. I thought that once I got to her—"

"You just ignored your mandated duty as a licensed child care director and did as you damn pleased!" He strode once around the office, then came back to stand before her.

"Don't you get it? This may be an international crime," his words came like bullets.

"Do you call this an international crime just because the missing child's from Zimbabwe?"

"That remains to be seen. But"—his voice became gentler and he spoke more slowly as he looked directly at her—"you should know, Hannah, we're not only talking here about the child's disappearance, grave as that is. Are you aware that last night at six thirty his father, Tapiwa Moyo, died, in what may or may not have been accident?"

Hannah blanched and slumped deep in her chair at this news. "Sheriff, I had no idea—I said good-bye to Tapiwa and Farai just before then. What happened?"

"A bicyclist, someone by the name of George Vincent, slammed him to the pavement, over at the Na Lis pizza stand. That's across from one of your buildings, isn't it?"

"Yes, it is," Hannah breathed.

"The lights on the stand went out—we don't know for sure before or after. The little boy was with his father when it happened, but when our cars and ambulance restored light to the scene, the boy had disappeared. Not a trace of him. "

"And Tapiwa died? Just from a fall?"

"Brainstem herniation, that's the term for it. He fell hard, and in such a way that his skull fractured. I could tell you more details—"

Her hand gestured to halt him. "No, I get it, Patrick." She straightened her back.

"His wife, Chipo, does she know her husband is dead? Is anyone with her?"

"We sent a car up there an hour ago after we got Mr. Moyo's home address from PTI."

"You did? Chipo has a terrible fear of anyone in uniform, Patrick. Did she actually let in the deputy you sent?"

"I haven't heard anything negative. The deputy is a black woman." He fidgeted with the top of his night stick. "Either she'll stay with Mrs. Moyo until we find the boy, or she'll make sure neighbors stand by. Hannah, I want you to come with me now, to headquarters."

"Why on earth?"

"You spent the night at Chipo's. That makes you a material witness to an aspect of this kidnapping."

"But why do you need me to come with you to headquarters?"

He sat down on the edge of Gina's chair, his body taut, and sighed.

"Even if this is an accidental death as the bicyclist claims, at the very least it was reckless disregard—his traveling at such high speed on the sidewalk, in the dark, where people were standing. Reckless disregard resulting in death is second degree murder. Then, as you know Mr. Moyo was a black man and Vincent's white—this could possibly be a hate crime. We've not been able to establish any connection between Vincent and Moyo."

His mouth tightened as he seemed to look inward. "We've

sighted three men around town this last week, men from Moyo's country. It's possible that for internal reasons we can't know, they may have wanted Moyo dead."

Again he circled her office. "So do you get the gravity here, Hannah?"

"Patrick, if I have to come with you now, of course I will. But I fail to see how my leaving this busy center, with over a hundred children, and teachers and parents who are worried and upset about what's happened, and all the usual jobs and deadlines to be accomplished, can be helpful to you—"

Her old fashioned, even schoolmarmish manner of speech and thinking had sometimes in the past been a comfort to Bronson, but today they were an extreme aggravation. "I need you to come with me now, Hannah." He opened the door to her office to usher her out.

"By the way, who was that really angry woman who just left? Nearly knocked me down when she went out. She was in melt-down!"

"One of the staff, Patrick. It's her regular mode."

"Anything to do with the Moyos?"

"She did say something about a missing child, just before you came. She's out of her mind with fear of losing her job here, so I don't know what to think."

"Give me her address and number—right now, please."

Hannah gave these to him, and he picked up her phone, punched in numbers. "Sims? Bronson speaking. Ms. Cooper was informed a quarter-hour ago about a missing child. As soon as you get this message, get over to Ms. Nefas' home. This might be what we're looking for."

"Be sure to tell Detective Sims about this when he interrogates you this morning. Any detail that might be relevant, we need to know it, do you understand?"

She instructed Gina to cancel the day's staff meeting and let Alexis know she wouldn't be at her office by eight thirty. The sheriff allowed her to drive her own car behind him downtown to his office, which made her feel encouraged that she might be permitted to return to work later in the day.

Once they reached headquarters, she gave a recorded statement in which she described her last sight of Tapiwa and Farai the night before and her subsequent night at Chipo's. She agreed to comply with Bronson's request that she would not leave the limits of the City of Pasadena until further notice. He allowed her to return to her office.

Halfway out the door she heard his bark. "Detective Sims is on his way to your center right now, so get yourself back over there ASAP."

49

Sekai meditated about how she would break the news of Ruvimbo's arrival to her friend's daughter as she chugged north on Allen Street. Such news could be difficult to receive, she knew, especially when it followed directly on the heels of fear. And her acquaintance with Chipo was minimal. She turned right on Villa and left on Roosevelt toward Chipo's unit. Though she'd never visited the student apartment complex, she had a general idea of its location somewhere on her right. The first sight that alerted her that she was close to her destination was a cluster of sheriff's cars, their flashing lights revolving.

Instantly she was a young woman again, watching Ian Smith's thugs drag men in her village from their huts. Their tall black boots gleamed; she saw khaki shirts with strange insignia, military caps above blank, in-turned gazes. Always these images would remain with her.

She wanted to accelerate and speed by. Then she realized how suspicious this might appear and, with an effort, instead continued her innocent-looking slow pace, cruising by the units without a glance. Once past them, she peered into her rearview mirror, seeing Chipo and a female deputy sheriff; the khaki uniform embraced and supported the limp, flowered form.

No way could she stop to carry out her mission—and she needed to be at work soon.

She turned her car southward and switched on the radio, catching a fragment of news. Thus did Sekai learn of Tapiwa's death.

50

If Hannah thought her return to the center from the sheriff's headquarters would comfort and ground her, her hopes were soon dashed. Gina greeted her at ten forty-five with a list of phone messages, including one from Joan asking to see her ASAP, and the news that Detective Sims from the sheriff's office would interview her at the center in fifteen minutes.

"Gina, please call Joan and tell her I'm not free this morning," Hannah asked.

She had a quarter of an hour, and she would take care of herself. She'd had no breakfast at Chipo's, so she helped herself to an apple from the kitchen and went to spend this fragment of time under the trees in Anne's fours yard, where she could enjoy the children's play around her.

As always, their activities engaged and strengthened her as almost nothing else could. What a joy to watch Angela, full of importance, playing the role of mechanic; her tiny fingers tightened imaginary bolts on the scooter wheels and oiled an invisible engine on a tricycle while Jimmy, who rode it, waited patiently. Children sometimes need gentle adult help to begin such imaginary activities. Sometimes, of course, a staff member's idea for dramatic play might not catch on at all, but clearly this one had succeeded. Hannah remembered how shy Angela had been a few months ago when she began at the center. *Look at her now!*

Then she noticed an incipient shoving match about to explode in another part of the yard, and saw Tony move, inconspicuous but fast, toward the two girls involved. His presence alone seemed to ease the tension from their bodies. Only a few months ago, Hannah recalled, Tony would have ignored the early warning signs of an incipient conflict until after the fact, then he'd race over to it full steam and start to bark at the kids. What a difference! Hannah couldn't help but feel pride in Tony's professional growth. She'd worked with him on alertness to impending struggles, and how to help the kids find effective ways to handle them.

"Young children are socially inexperienced," she'd told him. "They often provoke confrontations. Skillful teachers know how to help them learn to negotiate. Children can learn one of the most important lessons of life here: you can be mad or scared, and a second later you can be friends with the person you were mad at or scared of."

"Yeah, Hannah," he would mutter on these occasions. But he had heard!

A stranger approached the center's main entrance. Middle aged, heavy, but he moved with grace. Skin the color of smoke, short thick gray hair, and eyes that were sad but sharply observant. Hannah saw him knock on the door and wait respectfully until a teacher opened it and asked him his business. She swallowed the last of her apple and took a gulp of water as she rose to cross the yard to the entrance.

One of the aspects of the center that had always bothered Hannah was that the only access to her upstairs office led directly through a classroom. In her mind she tried to balance this inconvenience with the delightful intimacy of a homelike setting for the children. But at moments like this—and they were frequent—when strangers approached and interrupted teachers at their work, she felt her equanimity teeter.

She heard the sound of the stranger's deep, courteous voice and walked briskly but quietly through the play yard, as Tony had a few moments earlier, toward the center entrance.

"Yes, ma'am, I'm from the sheriff's office, to see Hannah Cooper, please." Clad in plain clothes, he held out his identification for the teacher to inspect.

"Thanks, he's expected. You're Detective Sims?" Hannah realized as she spoke that she should have waited for him to identify himself before she mentioned the name Bronson had given her. However, the ID he proffered confirmed the name: Detective Donald Sims of the Los Angeles County Sheriff's Department. She motioned him in and took him quickly through the threes room, where nap preparations were going on, then upstairs to her office.

51

"Where might we talk alone?" Sims asked Hannah. Gina worked at her desk, and a parent and teacher seated in metal chairs waited just outside the office.

Given the panicky state of the staff after Tapiwa's sudden death, Hannah knew that the mere presence of a stranger speaking with her could start rumors. She spoke in as everyday a tone as she could. "No one's in the staff break room, Mr. Sims," she said, "and we can try to talk there. About how long do you think we'll need?"

"Probably not more than thirty minutes this time, ma'am." His voice matched hers in evenness.

"Gina, I'll be free in half an hour," Hannah told the bookkeeper, including the two in the hallway in her glance as she spoke. She led Detective Sims down the hall to the cramped staff break area. Its door had been removed long ago. The room, smaller even than the office, was crammed with a sofa, upholstered chairs, and several floor cushions. Weekly staff meetings were held here, with younger and more limber teachers sitting on the floor; the rest of the week it served for smaller meetings and as a siesta or lunch space during staff breaks.

"Ms. Cooper, I'm here, as you know, to find out what I can about the Farai Moyo case," Sims began. He had seated himself inside the room. Hannah sat sideways on the sofa, facing him and with her back to the open doorway and hall so that anyone passing could see her occupied with Sims and, she hoped, proceed to the office.

"So, to get down to it, do you have any idea who might have taken the boy last night?"

She heard kind undertones in Sims' deep, even gruff voice.

"I've thought hard about Farai ever since his mother called me shortly after eleven last night. At first Chipo and I thought Farai might be at the apartment where Elaine Sark lives, near campus. Elaine's—"

"We're in communication with Elaine."

"Oh?" Hannah's eyebrows stretched upward as her eyes widened. "Well, she was one person I thought might possibly have information about Farai's whereabouts."

"Any other thoughts?" Sims made brief penciled notes on a battered blue spiral notebook he'd pulled from his rear pocket.

"Would you like a larger notepad, Mr. Sims, and a pen?" Their conversation was speeding faster than Hannah felt comfortable with.

He gave her a patient look. "No thanks, ma'am, this little notebook works just fine for me, fits into my pocket, easy to pull out." He parked the stubby pencil behind his right ear and cocked his large head toward her in an almost comically exaggerated listening position. A moment of silence ensued, in which Hannah remembered he'd asked her a question.

"Oh—any other thoughts you asked me, didn't you, Mr. Sims. Yes, some other people do come to mind. One is Joan Nefas, a teacher on our staff. She told me this morning that she has some important information about one of our children, and tried to use it to bargain with me to keep her job here. This is confidential information, of course—"

"Excuse me, Ms. Cooper," he interrupted, "but we're investigating a kidnap here, tied to a possible murder. We need to know every detail about anyone who may be responsible, confidential or not." He closed his eyes, straightened his shoulders.

"Of course, we'll do our best to maintain confidentiality." He paused. "Right now I need to know why this Ms. Nefas is about to lose her job here. Can you tell me?"

Hannah felt her mind open as she realized that her normal guidelines of professional discretion, of not sharing personal information, no longer applied in this urgent situation. It was a freeing moment for her.

"Without going into all that led up to our decision to dismiss Joan tomorrow, Detective Sims," she told him, "the bottom line is that four days ago, a parent saw her inflict physical pain on a child in her care. State law requires in such a case that the action be reported and the teacher dismissed. This is the first time at our center—"

"Anything else I should know about Ms. Nefas? For instance, have you noted previous tendencies toward child abuse?"

"No, not physical abuse, Detective Sims. But besides the fact that she hinted strongly this morning at having information, it's also true that some years back, before I came here, when Joan was a much less experienced teacher, she decided one evening to take a child home with her."

"How could that be?" His forehead tightened as he cocked his head.

"Apparently, when his parents didn't arrive to pick him up, Joan decided to take him home for the night instead of calling the director."

"How do you know this?" Sims scratched the back of his head.

"From her file."

"Hmm. What happened then?"

"The father reached the director at home a couple of hours after closing time, demanding to know what she'd done with his son. He told her he and the child's mother each thought the other would pick up the boy.

"The director called Joan and learned what had happened. Joan had given the child dinner, bathed him, and tucked him into a makeshift bed in her living room—and notified no one. She acted highly unprofessionally, against our policies, and illegally. She insisted she only had the child's good at heart."

Sims crossed his arms and leaned back. "Why would a teacher do a thing like that?"

Hannah's words came slowly as she thought out her answer. "I think she may have chosen to ignore center policies because she felt angry at the parents for what she perceived as neglect of their son. New teachers sometimes get a kind of God complex, where they feel they know a child's needs better than do his parents."

"Does Joan have children of her own?"

"No, and you're right, Mr. Sims. That could have been part of the serious error in judgment she made. Anyway, the parents were embarrassed because they hadn't picked up their son, and they were fond of Joan and trusted her, so they were willing to pass over the incident.

"The next day Joan and the director met with the head of our board personnel committee at that time, and they carefully reviewed the staff policies together. Joan apologized, and they decided to keep her on."

Sims considered. "Would you have made the decision to keep her on the staff, Ms. Cooper, if you'd been here at the time?"

"Joan has strengths as a teacher, and promising teachers are hard to find. I'm not sure what my decision would have been." Hannah searched the detective's impassive face for understanding but could read nothing.

"This day care situation's so different from what would happen with an older child, say, at an elementary school," he said, "and I can't wrap my mind around what you've told me. This happened when again?"

"In the early eighties, Detective Sims. You have to understand how much more legalistic everything's gotten since then. Back then parents usually trusted their child's caregiver. It was before the McMartin case. Things were much more relaxed. No routine fingerprinting of all child care personnel back then, Detective Sims, no criminal checks. A different time."

She hated even to mention the McMartin child care home in Manhattan Beach, California, where accusations of sexual molestation were made in the mid-eighties. National hysteria had followed. After years of prosecution and trials, charges were dropped against all accused staff members at the McMartin child care home, but not before some of its staff had spent time in jail. Some still insist the grounds for closing the home were valid.

"Do you think Joan might actually have repeated the action you just told me about and taken Farai home with her?"

"I know he left the center at the end of the day with his father, so Joan certainly did not take Farai at that time. But I also know she knows something and was trying to bargain with me about it this morning when Sheriff Bronson interrupted us. She knows she's to be terminated tomorrow and she's desperate."

Sims nodded, ran his hand through his hair. He took the pencil stub from behind his ear and made another note.

"Do you have any other thoughts about who might be responsible for the boy's disappearance?"

"Well—you'll think this is crazy, but I'll tell you anyway—a parent at our center, Sue Bowles, who's going through some very hard changes right now, told me a couple of months ago that she'd like to adopt Farai, take him home to live with her and her son. She felt extremely critical of his mother and wanted to 'rescue' Farai from her.

"And—" Hannah's new perception kicked in again. "Sue's been under the care of a therapist for her depression, and the medications she's been given often cloud her mind. It's just possible I suppose, that if she were at the pizza stand last night, she might have taken the boy home with her."

She grew silent, as did he as he scrawled out a few more notes. Then, "Any other thoughts, Ms. Cooper?"

She cleared her throat.

"My last thought's even more farfetched. It's about a group of men—two young, one older. We think they're from Zimbabwe. They've been seen around town this week. They harassed Chipo yesterday, wanted to see Tapiwa. It's possible Tapiwa's death might have been political."

Her voice shook. Reading about such things in the papers felt way different from the possibility of their happening to a young father at her child care center. Suddenly her body jerked as a new thought broke through her mind.

"Is it possible the boy is held hostage?"

She's so innocent. "We don't know." Sims nodded and slowly rose to his feet. "Ms. Cooper, thanks for your help on this very painful matter." He stood before her. "I'm afraid our 'thirty minutes' stretched into almost an hour, but it's been useful. What you've told me may be helpful. I'd like you to give me phone numbers and addresses for Joan Nefas and Sue Bowles."

"What about the three men?"

"I'm not at liberty to discuss them, Ms. Cooper, but I thank you again for the information. I'll get back to you if I need anything more. I'd like you to call me with anything at all that looks to you like it might help us find the boy. I would also like you to come in to headquarters tomorrow morning for further questioning."

Hannah rose a little stiffly. She gave Sims the phone numbers and received from him his personal twenty-four-hour number. Each promised to call the other with questions or news of Farai. Hannah felt relief at no longer being constrained to go through Drabb. They shook hands warmly.

She noted how quietly Sims descended the stairs toward the room full of sleeping children below. Might he be a grandfather?

In the office three people now awaited her. There would be no catnap any time soon.

52

Detective Donald Sims entered the Computer Shack at twelve noon. He showed Ben his badge.

Without Sims asking, Ben went over to the door, turned the "Open" sign on it to "Closed," set the little "back by ..." clock to twelve twenty, turned out the store lights, and motioned Sims to the repair area in back.

"Usually my assistant's back here, but he phoned in sick this morning," Ben told Sims. "I think I know what's really bothering him though, and it's got everything to do with why you're here, sir."

"What are you getting at?" Sims asked, seating himself on George's stool, the only place to sit in this part of the shop. Ben leaned against the door jamb.

"Well, for starters, he accidentally killed a man last night, right? That's got to shake anybody up. But his luck's not been good lately, and he already seemed pretty down in the mouth."

"Can you tell me a little more about that?" Sims inquired.

"Hell, he don't talk much about his personal life. But I know he lives alone now and don't seem to have friends or go out much. He don't fit in very well. Come here from Missouri to go to Pasadena Tech, but didn't make it. Owes money there, student loans, whatever. But he's a good worker, knows his stuff! Hey, will he need a character reference, or whatever? I could offer that. His work record here's sound. Said in the paper he'd probably be released after his arraignment this morning. Is that what happened?"

"Yeah, he's released, but he's to stay in town while we check some of the details."

Ben's eyes widened, and even his ears appeared to open. "Like what?"

"Can you tell me if a group of black men, not dressed Western style, appeared in your shop recently?"

Ben's voice rose in surprise. "Yes, they were here yesterday afternoon. They needed a cell phone battery. You don't see cell phones here too much, though they're coming in big and pretty soon everyone will have one—I hear in China and even Africa they have them already."

"Did you notice anything suspicious about the men?"

"No, can't say I did. George acted suspicious, but he's always suspicious of blacks—no offense, sir."

"None taken." Sims smiled at Ben, meeting his eyes. His tone resumed its briskness. "Did George talk alone with these men at any time you can remember?"

"Well, yeah, come to think of it, he could have! He were alone with them when I went out to talk to Maya—that's my wife. And he seemed real shaky when I came back in. You don't think—"

"I don't think what?"

"You don't think they *hired* him to do that killing, do you?"

"That's an interesting idea, Ben." Sims closed his eyes and tipped back his head as his lips tightened.

A short silence.

"Guess I've seen too much TV, huh?"

"We all have. Don't worry about it. Thanks for your help. We'll call if we need to talk with you again, okay? I think that's all I need to know for now."

And with a handshake, Detective Sims left Ben's shop.

53

At twelve forty-five Detective Sims drove his unmarked Chevrolet Impala to the mobile park where Joan Nefas lived. He thought about Hannah: *what a caring woman, yet so sheltered.* Children were kidnapped in his world, but she seemed to regard Farai Moyo's disappearance as unique. If only it were, he sighed to himself.

The mobile park appeared well maintained, the units landscaped and recently painted. Small garden areas in front of each spoke of the individuals who owned them: hanging chimes and a bird bath at one, "Beware the Cat" sign on a graveled area at another, luxuriant winter-blooming roses at a third. Unit numbers were clearly displayed, and Sims easily found Joan's home, with potted geraniums edging the path to the entrance, a small shade tree to one side, and under it, a long hammock. He could glimpse a woman's lanky figure inside the kitchen to the left of the front door, which stood ajar. He parked his unmarked car around a curve just beyond her unit, noticing her neighbor, a wizened man in beret and thick woolen pants and shirt, on his knees in the small vegetable garden that took up all the space between the road and his mobile home. Sims walked back to Joan's and up the few steps from the sidewalk.

He tapped on the open door, stepped well back from it, and announced, "Ms Nefas? Detective Sims on official business," extending his right arm and holding out his identification in his open hand.

Something inside dropped loudly—a spoon onto the counter? Or maybe onto the floor? He couldn't be sure, but whatever it was, it didn't break. A woman hurried toward him, her features tight, hostile. He knew her dilemma: should she invite him inside, where neighbors couldn't see or hear, or should she stand outside with him, in view of anyone who looked out a window or passed by? The fear of law officers, based on actual police abuse and also on misunderstanding—he encountered it every day. It played a part in the majority of his work situations, and he'd been trained, and learned well, how to operate within it. It wasn't usually possible to change it.

"We could talk inside, ma'am, with your door open as you had it. It should take only a few minutes."

She gave an abrupt nod, turned her back, and moved into the sitting room to the right of the door. He entered behind her at a distance, the door now wide open behind him.

"Let me tell you why I've come," he began. "I don't know if you've heard, or seen the papers this morning, but the father of one of the children at the center where you work died last night in an accident, and his son's missing."

He noted her lack of any response as he looked around the room. Almost every horizontal surface overflowed with stacks of mail, magazines, and loose papers. The windows were dusty, and wisps of spider webs clung to and dangled from the ceiling. Only the sofa, across from a thirteen-inch television, was bare.

"I talked with your boss, Hannah Cooper, this morning,

and she gave me to understand that the boy's in your class, Ms. Nefas. Farai Moyo is his name."

Joan nodded. "Yes, Farai's in my class. Though I'm not at the center this week, as Hannah may have told you. Why are you interrogating me?"

"Ms Cooper mentioned you told her this morning that you had some important information—she said you didn't say exactly about what. We're following every lead, ma'am, to find this boy before he's possibly hurt, or worse."

Joan displayed no concern. Her eyes shone feverishly. "Have you ever had your job on the line, Mr. Sims? I said whatever I could this morning to Hannah, to keep my position. I know nothing about Farai's disappearance. I didn't even go to the center yesterday—I spent the day with friends who'd vouch for that. Now do you think I could have my lunch? I have something I need to do this afternoon."

"So you lied to Hannah this morning about knowledge of important information?"

"What are you, a judge? I suppose you never tell anything but the absolute truth?"

"But this particular lie? How did you come up with this particular lie, Ms. Nefas?"

"Actually, it was easy. To bargain with Hannah is like taking candy from a baby, Mr. Sims. She's one of those trusting souls, never had it hard like me. I heard her on the phone when I walked in. Something urgent, she said. I knew right away it had to be a child in trouble. So I just faked that I had useful information. She fell for it. I'd've gotten my job back then and there, if that damn sheriff hadn't walked in."

Sims stood. "You must understand, Ms. Nefas, that this child's life may be in danger. I may need to question you further in the future."

"I certainly hope not. I've got way too much on my mind right now." She stood up and moved ahead of him out the open front door. He followed her outside.

"I like your geraniums, Ms. Nefas," he told her as he turned up the road toward his car.

Bronson's message to Sims had been delayed by the dispatcher. Sims thought about her as he drove to headquarters. She was in a bad place. And disturbed. He wished he could slap a fifty-one-fifty on her and hold her for seventy-two hours, or just until she calmed down a little and felt better, but he had no legal grounds to do that. He'd seen it so many times: a person in her state of mind ended up hurting someone. No wonder Bronson had told him to check her out, pronto. Sims hoped she wouldn't explode.

54

Gina must have stepped out on an errand, and after half an hour or so, Hannah settled the questions and concerns of those who'd waited in the office, now blessedly empty. Hannah's mind hummed. She had a sudden realization that she and Sims had never even discussed Tapiwa's death, whether accidental or otherwise. They'd stayed entirely with possibilities about the whereabouts of Farai, probing into who might have snatched the boy the night before.

Well, she, too, would try to focus her thoughts; she would mourn Tapiwa later. Maybe they could still save the boy. An image of Farai flashed across her mind, a rag stuffed in his mouth, his hands and feet tied, curled up in the trunk of a car, terrified. She forced it away. Such thoughts only clouded her brain, and she desperately needed whatever brain she had available to her.

Of the possibilities she'd mentioned to Sims—Elaine, Joan, Sue, the three African men—who did she think the most likely? Though she didn't know Elaine, she nevertheless considered her a possible source of information. Since state law required that child care centers have on file a way to reach both parents of each child, she had Elaine's phone number. Of late Tapiwa had been reachable only at Elaine's.

Should she call this woman she had never met or even seen and ask her what she might know about last night? Chipo had told her that Elaine could be formidably foul-mouthed, even abusive, and Hannah didn't relish the thought of provoking a useless tirade. But she shook her head at this cowardly thought, looked up Elaine's number, and punched in the digits before she could invent other reasons for not acting right away.

"Yes?" Hoarse voice.

"Elaine Sark?"

"Yes."

"Elaine, I'm Hannah Cooper, over at the Child Development Center. I'm sorry about the nasty shock you've had. I'm calling about Farai, Tapiwa's son." Should she allude to Chipo's desperate call to Elaine the night before? Probably unwise to do that.

"You may not know that Farai disappeared last night when his dad was killed. No one knows where he is, and—"

"Ms. Cooper, I do know that. Tapiwa's wife called me last night. I yelled at her, I'm afraid. I was upset when Tapiwa didn't show up to get his things, and then she woke me up right after I finally fell asleep. As I told her, I have no idea where the boy is. The sheriff's office has been after me too. They called this morning. I think maybe they've bugged my phone—"

That's why she's so civil to me, Hannah realized.

"This is all pretty scary, Ms. Cooper, isn't it? Tapiwa's dead and his son's missing. Some guys from his country looked for him yesterday. This morning I told the sheriff that, but he already seemed to know about it. He wouldn't tell me anything though. When Tapiwa moved in with me last month, I had no idea ..." Her voice trailed into heavy silence and Hannah thought she might hang up.

"I have lab in a few minutes, and I'm afraid to leave the apartment," Elaine resumed. "My shades are pulled and I've got a chair under my front doorknob. The sheriff said to call if we saw any sign of those guys—"

Hannah wanted to comfort this girl in her misery; she understood it was all the sharper because Elaine had brought it on herself. But Hannah knew that right now every second might decide whether Farai lived. She gave Elaine the center's number, asked her to call if she learned anything that could be helpful, and promised to do the same for her. "Call me any time, Elaine, any time at all," she told her, and Elaine responded, "Drop on by if you have a free minute, Hannah."

Was this scared girl the same woman who'd seduced Tapiwa and yelled at his wife? On her list she jotted "believably knows nothing about F."

Joan had told her she had information. Had Joan made that up? Was the information even about Farai? Would Detective Sims extract from Joan whatever she knew? It should be easier for him than for her to do that, what with Joan's job issue in the way. Hannah resolved to put aside the possibility of Joan for now. Next to Joan's name on her list, she wrote, "wait for Sims."

Okay, what about Sue, Hannah mused. *She lives fairly close, and I could just go to her bungalow. She's usually home during the day trying to write her dissertation—or asleep, poor woman.*

Where was Gina? Hannah jotted her a note, "Gina—Gone on a quick visit to Sue B. Back soon, H." She added the time, one thirty, and put the note on Gina's desk with a ruler over it so that only Gina's name showed. The early-morning clouds had receded and sun shone here and there, casting shadows below the oak tree beneath her window. Nevertheless, she picked up a light jacket from the hook on the back of the office door as she headed for the stairs.

For a wonder, no staff member accosted her as she made her way toward the exit to her car: no one asked her whether she could get a sub for them the next day at ten, or two thirty, or four o'clock, expecting her to remember this and deal with it when she returned to her office. Nap time music played downstairs—Mozart, she thought. Before she left she tiptoed into Joan's fours room. The children, apparently not upset by Joan's absence, sang a song Hannah didn't know, something about snowflakes. Hannah took a look at the parent sign-in-sign-out sheet, and learned that William Brost had signed out Aaron the previous evening at five twenty p.m. Hannah knew that William's name was on file as an approved pick-up person for the boy. She opened the door to the play yard, crossed it, then opened the outside gate.

Not for the first time, security precautions entered her mind. Anyone knowledgeable about the center could enter from the street during the day and burst in to snatch a child or rake a classroom with gunfire, as had happened several times in California within the last few years. The gates had been constructed in 1972 with the sole idea of keeping children safe inside, away from the busy street outside. The latches were above a child's reach. The gates had been constructed with the underlying, unspoken assumption that the world values and cherishes children. The gates couldn't keep out crazy adults.

Hannah had seen the entrances to recently built child care centers in Los Angeles' inner city—heavy metal doors, like those to the vault in her bank, with combinations that changed daily and that parents had to remember, doors that clanged and reverberated against solid metal fences. She had resisted turning her center into a fortress, feeling that both children and parents needed the exterior to be warm, open, and inviting.

Would she find Sue in? Would Bronson object to her going directly to Sue, even though her motive of possibly saving Farai should be clear?

55

Sims' visit made little impression on Joan. Her job was her sole focus now. In her earliest memories, she'd craved the stability and peace of mind that were nonexistent in her crowded New Jersey scrub farm home. The enforced idleness of the last few days had only increased the value of her job for her, and she felt frantic at the thought of no work world to go to each morning, no paycheck twice a month, no young parents and staff looking up to her.

She simply had to keep her job. She would *make* them let her keep her job. When Sims left she ate her sandwich without tasting it, standing up in her kitchen—Wonder Bread and peanut butter, washed down with fruit punch. She'd never had to worry about metabolizing what she ate; it seemed to pour off her body. Her thoughts darted wildly as she stood motionless for what seemed a long time but was actually only five minutes.

A plan began to form for her. She did, after all, have some important information, and it was crucial that she use it now, this minute, to save her job, save her life.

Her clenched body came alive at last. She ran to her phone

and began rummaging through her center directory pages for Sekai's address. Her trembling fingers slowed her search; the thin pages wrinkled and tore as she turned them. Ah! She found it: 503 North Wilson, less than a mile from the center. Then she searched her city phone directory for the business phone of Andrew Chin and jotted it down. She swooped up her car keys, raced out the door, ran back and locked it, and hurried to her Studebaker, which was parked in front. The passenger and back seats were full of crumpled Reese's Peanut Butter Cup wrappers, soggy tissues, apple cores, smelly plastic containers, and jumbo popcorn and soft drink cups. Joan revved up the engine, accelerated, then made a squealing U-turn, splattering mud onto the sidewalks, and exited the mobile home park.

She turned west on Colorado Boulevard, sped to Wilson, and headed north. "Roo-vim-bo, Roo-vim-bo," she repeated as she drove. Sekai had mentioned her friend's name this morning, and Joan had a talent for names—you had to, when you worked with at least thirty children each year, with parents' and siblings' names to memorize as well.

No parking spots! That Cadillac, hogging two spots. She should—that one over there? No! No! There *couldn't* be no parking, not now. She had to find a spot. She couldn't lose everything because of parking unavailability. There! Tail lights—pick-up backing out! She yanked the wheel to the right, barely missed the truck's bumper. The driver yelled. Joan had already grabbed her bag.

But as abruptly as she'd swerved into the spot thirty seconds earlier, she now froze. "Wait a minute, Joan," she told herself. "Calm down. You need to be cool and convincing for this." Three deep breaths.

"Okay, I'm as ready as I'll ever be." She slipped into the normally locked apartment building as someone from inside emerged from the front door, then took the elevator to the second floor and knocked at number 112.

Light footsteps perforated the silence inside. No further sound, and the door remained closed.

"Ruvimbo," she called, "I'm Joan Nefas. Sekai sent me to take Farai to my home. She'll meet us there after work. She thought someone was watching her, so she didn't want to come back here now."

Still no sound.

"Ruvimbo, I'm Farai's teacher at the center. I'm a safe person. Ask him—he'll tell you." Joan's tone did not reveal her desperation. Did she hear whispers on the other side?

An older woman's voice spoke through the door. "Farai is safe here with me. We do not need you to take care of him."

Joan considered. *Not* what she wanted, but maybe it would work anyway. And once the door was open, she could size things up, maybe even get Farai away from the old biddy.

"All right," she called, "but I have something here that Sekai gave me for you." Metal bolts rasped; a key turned, and the door opened a thin crack. Farai had opened it; his grandmother had both arms clenched around his body, and her brown-eyed gaze stabbed straight into Joan's green eyes, went right through Joan and beyond her.

"Hello, Farai," Joan greeted the boy in her best teacherly tone, squatting to his level. Then she stood and strode purposefully into Sekai's apartment.

"Why haven't you been at the center since Monday?" Farai asked her. How like him to go right to the heart of the matter.

"I couldn't, but I hope to be back there very soon," she responded, "and you can help me do that by coming with me now, Farai."

The grandmother had not relaxed her grip on him, Joan saw, and she mentally came to terms with this new and unexpected reality. Maybe this would work better for her than her original plan. She spoke with authority. "Hold Farai if you wish. I know you've come a long distance to see him."

She settled the older woman and Farai in Sekai's small

sitting room as if it were her own, and called the office of Andrew Chin, PCDC's board president and father of Song Lee in her fours group.

"Andrew, this is Joan Nefas from PCDC," she began. "I'm not calling about Song Lee. Your precious little darling is okay as far as I know, though your stupid board kept me from taking care of her and protecting her this week. Just kidding, Andrew, sorry. I'm calling you about Farai Moyo. I guess you know what happened to his father last night, and that Farai's missing? Well, I have the child with me, Andrew, safe and sound. Promise me my job back, and no harm will come to him.

"No, I won't bring him to the center, Andrew. You need to come and get him. And no, I won't tell you where we are. I'll call you again in one hour, and unless I get my job back, I can't promise that Farai will be safe. Got that?

"Okay, I'll talk to you again at three o'clock, Andrew. Bye now."

56

Ruvimbo sat close to Farai, gripping him tightly with both hands. Who was this Andrew? Would he come and rescue them? She looked into Farai's eyes and gave him a close-lipped smile as she prayed for their safe deliverance. He returned the gaze and the fleeting smile.

"Can I ask you something, *Ambuya?*" he whispered in Shona.

She nodded and cocked her head.

"How's Coomi?"

She almost "lost it," as Sekai had said she might. "Coomi's just fine, and he wags his tail and sends you his love," she whispered back in Shona.

Together, grandmother and grandson were invincible, bound together in their own world at this tense time. They would be ready for whatever might happen next with the strange, sinister woman.

57

As she drove north to Sue's backyard bungalow, Hannah considered how best to approach the subject of Farai's disappearance. She knew Aaron was presently at the center; she'd glimpsed him at morning snack. Sue would probably be alone, as she'd made few friends during her difficult first year here. Perhaps she would be asleep. Sue had been forthright with Hannah about her depressions and sleep deprivation. "I'm working on it, Hannah," she'd told her, "and Phyllis is working with me. I'll be okay, I know. It just takes time."

I'll knock and then enter, even if I don't get a response—but what will I say to her, what do I want to know? I want to know if she somehow abducted Farai and brought him to her home last night, if she's hidden him there, carrying out those strange words of hers last fall about giving Farai a "stable home." I know she's suffered delusions these last months, poor woman, but would she really go this far?

And how could Sue have spirited Farai away from the scene of last night's accident? Preposterous, the whole idea.

But wait. Aaron had been with William at Sue's home. Sue

might have been at the pizza stand alone, and if so, she could have grabbed Farai after the accident.

But how could she have kept him overnight, unbeknownst to Aaron—how could she possibly have done that? As for Farai, Hannah knew that children will accept a lot without question once they trust someone, but surely this would have been too much; Farai, with no word from Chipo, could never have been kept quiet overnight at Sue's.

At one forty-five, she turned into the graveled driveway that led past the larger house in front, and drove slowly to its end. Rutted puddles reflected patches of clouds against a blue sky. She avoided the mud, maneuvered so the car pointed toward the street, and parked.

The wild cry of a hawk and the occasional two notes of a towhee, a tone apart, rang out nearby. She could depend on these sounds to soothe her anxieties and renew her spirits. She noted with additional pleasure that Sue's alyssum, and even birds of paradise, were in bud or blooming. This seemed a tender, secure little world, even though she knew differently.

Every blind at every window was drawn.

She walked gingerly around the puddles, made her way to Sue's door, and knocked gently, then with more force. Sue's faint voice answered the second knock. Hannah couldn't distinguish her words. She turned the tarnished brass doorknob and peered in. In the dim light she saw Sue at her table, head raised, a mug before her, an empty plate with a fork beside her, and dead flowers in a glass jar. It appeared she'd been there quite a while, perhaps with her head on her arms. She looked up at Hannah.

"I apologize, breaking in on you like this," Hannah began. "We've had a sad thing happen to one of our center families, and I thought just maybe you could shed some light on it." She couldn't bring herself to name Farai or Tapiwa right away, but she knew she had to.

"Shed some light? I sure don't have much of that these days,

Hannah, but tell me the problem. Who knows, maybe it'll break my writer's block—maybe I'll at least open my computer." She gestured toward the dusty desk across the room with its laptop, unevenly stacked books, and sheaf of papers.

"Aaron will tell you when he comes home this evening— Farai's not at the center today. What it is, is—what it is, Sue, is"—Hannah's words came in a rush—"no one knows where Farai is. He just disappeared into thin air last night after Tapiwa picked him up." She still couldn't bring herself to tell Sue about Tapiwa's death. "I know how close you are to Farai, and I wondered—"

"Oh Hannah, that's terrible! Where could he possibly be? Of course you've tried Chipo? And the woman Tapiwa's staying with? But did you think that I—"

Her face screwed up in puzzlement. "I love that boy, Hannah, and I know I told you I wished he could live with Aaron and me, but I wouldn't—" Her voice grew hoarse. "I wouldn't take a child from his mother without her knowing." Her eyes traveled across the room to a photo of Alan with Sophie in his arms. "I would not do that."

She shifted in her chair, signifying a change in the direction of her thoughts, then blurted, "I was there when it happened last night."

Hannah stopped breathing.

"You were there when Tapiwa was knocked down? But your name's not been mentioned, Sue. How did you—"

"I'd asked William to pick up Aaron while I got pizza at the Na Li stand, for the three of us."

"So you were at the stand when the accident happened?"

"I was terrified, Hannah. I was standing right next to Farai and his dad. I heard this loud crash—horrible—the lights went out—I heard Tapiwa thud on the sidewalk—" Her body bent double as she relived the shock.

"I reached for Farai—"

Hannah went to Sue and stood before her as Sue continued,

"Farai *wasn't there anymore*, Hannah. Like when Sophie died, only not even his body was there. I'm so ashamed."

"Ashamed? Why on earth?"

"Ashamed because all of a sudden I had this huge need to hold Aaron and never let him go." Her voice trembled, and she waited a moment to continue.

"I didn't wait to see how Tapiwa and Farai were—I didn't wait for Farai to be found—I didn't wait for the sheriff or anything. The next thing I remember is gunning my engine up El Molino and over to this little home of ours. I ran in, grabbed Aaron, and held him for the longest time."

In spite of her emotion, a faint smile appeared at the memory of her behavior. "I didn't want to tell William about the accident in front of Aaron, so I told him I needed to be alone with my son, and he left. I slept with Aaron all night."

"You were able to sleep?"

"Actually no, but Aaron did, and I lay next to him and just felt so grateful to hear his breath."

Hannah's eyes softened. "It must have been hard for you to separate from him this morning at the center."

"Yes and no, Hannah. Have I ever told you how grateful I am for this warm, loving place he goes to every weekday? I think I've taken it for granted! PCDC's such a blessing for the children, and all of us parents."

Hannah knew for certain now that in terms of information about Farai's disappearance, her visit had been useless. She'd thought that if she could actually see Sue face to face and look around her home, she'd be better able to reassure herself. Her visit had served its purpose in that she now knew beyond all doubt that Sue knew nothing of Farai's whereabouts. Now she needed to extricate herself as kindly as possible and return to the center.

"I'm sorry," she said lamely. "About Farai, I shouldn't have suggested—" She paused, tried another tack: "You're often in my thoughts, Sue. This has got to be the hardest few months you'll live in your entire life. You lost your baby, your husband goes away when you most need him, and then last night you're right there when Tapiwa's killed and Farai disappears."

"Tapiwa did die? Oh, I knew it in my bones," Sue wailed as the tears she had waited for so long began to flow.

"I wish you had your dad or mother or an aunt or someone who's known you a long time, someone from back home, here with you now. Isn't there someone who might come?" Hannah laid a gentle hand on Sue's arm.

Sue looked directly at Hannah for a moment, then dropped her eyes. "Really not. Back home, they have their own problems or they're working, or both. Alan will be home soon. And William's been a good friend to Aaron and me; we'll probably always be friends." She opened her mouth as if on the verge of confiding something more, but closed it again.

As suddenly as they'd begun, her tears ceased and her voice took on new energy. "But right now I'm thinking of Chipo. She must be in deep pain. D'you think I could help her in some way?"

Hannah considered. "This will sound silly, but I'm big on chicken soup. It can do a lot," Hannah chuckled faintly at the concept. "Or something like chicken soup. Do you have anything in the kitchen you could make for her and take to her home? I'm sure that friends do that for each other in Zimbabwe as well as here."

Sue straightened, then stood. "I've got soup in cans and parsley in the garden to spruce it up. Thanks for the idea, Hannah, I'll try it. Chipo must trust me a little, or she wouldn't've let Farai visit here in the past. Maybe she'll let me sit with her now. "

Hannah had spent more time than she meant to. She told Sue good-bye, wished her a good outcome for her visit to Chipo, and headed outside. As she opened the car door, Sue ran out. "Hannah! It's Andrew Chin on the phone! It's urgent he says!"

58

"My God, Hannah, I'm so glad to reach you. They told me at the center you were here. I've had a call from Joan. She's out of her head. She says she's got Farai with her and that she'll return him only in exchange for getting her job back."

"How terrible! Where is she, Andrew?"

"She wouldn't say. I called Sheriff Bronson; he checked her home, and she's not there. Bronson said you might know where Joan could be. She said she'd call back at three o'clock—that's only thirty minutes away—and she won't guarantee Farai's safety after that time. Hannah, have you any idea where she might be?"

"I'm thinking, Andrew, thinking hard. Joan made some obscure remarks to me this morning." Hannah tapped the receiver with her index fingernail as she tried to recall. Something about a child who didn't come home last night, and a mother who didn't know *her* mother was here—"

"*In fact, my mother's dearest friend ...*" Hannah recalled Chipo's words of last fall.

"Andrew, you have your center directory? Good! I'll head to Sekai Turino's apartment on North Wilson right now. It's not far from where I am. Please, call Detective Sims, and I'll meet you both there. Oh! Andrew—bring Sekai's phone number with you too." She pulled Sims's card from her pocket and read the number to Andrew, then thrust the cordless phone into Sue's hands.

"No time for explanations, Sue," she called back to the younger woman. "I think we may have found our boy. Pray for us!" She hit the accelerator and disappeared, gravel spurting on blossoms.

Sue moved as quickly as Hannah had. She grabbed a sprig of parsley, a can of soup, and her purse, leaped into her car, and headed for Chipo's.

59

Elaine sat in her apartment, ruminating. She'd skipped her lab this afternoon, which was unheard of for her. Now she tried to quell her fears and think things through, a skill she felt she possessed. But the fears still gripped her. She revisited Tapiwa's face, so warm and open when he'd first come to her, then increasingly strained, then dark and set when he'd told her yesterday he wouldn't return. Why did she feel scared? Because of the violence visited on him, perhaps? That middle-of-the-night phone call last month: would more of these come her way?

And why did she feel guilty? Just because she intimately knew both the killer and the killed? No, it was just a horrible, random coincidence. Tapiwa's death had nothing to do with her.

When Hannah had phoned her in the early afternoon she'd felt physical relief; her legs trembled and she had to sit down as she talked with Hannah and implored her to come over. What had Hannah said in response to her plea? Something about maybe later this afternoon.

Elaine paced back and forth, back and forth. After a time she looked at her watch. Three thirty. She'd go downstairs and wait for Hannah. Surely she would come.

60

Sue arrived at Chipo's at two forty and came upon a strange sight. Chipo sat stiffly on Farai's bed, her eyes twice their normal size, straining to hear a sound, either from the pay phone outside or from the walkie-talkie held by the black female sheriff's deputy, who sat beside her. Though they were not talking, the two women nevertheless appeared to understand one another. The deputy kept her firm, compassionate gaze on Chipo, who seemed to have set aside, at least for now, her deep-rooted terror of those in uniform.

"I heard about Farai, and I want to be with you, Chipo," Sue began.

But the faint crackle of the deputy's walkie-talkie sounded before she could continue. The deputy's eyes came to life as she listened and responded, "Yes, I'll bring her right over. Is the child safe?"

Chipo started violently and stared deeply at her companion, who turned to her with a relieved expression, saying, "He's okay, Ms. Moyo. He's at the home of Sekai Turino. Let's go there, *now.*"

Chipo, already at the door, turned and glanced at Sue. "My friend may come too?"

The deputy nodded and beckoned Chipo to her official car. The three women ignored the neighbors who ran out to ask the latest news. Sue hurried to her Dodge and fell in behind the other car.

As they crept along the mile-and-a-half journey through the heavy mid-afternoon traffic, Chipo pictured her son. She saw him bursting with excitement the day he'd arrived at the center, and again in November, intent and focused as he drilled and hammered the block of wood clamped to the outdoor carpentry table. She saw him rolling with Aaron in a pile of liquid amber leaves on campus. She pictured him laughing out loud at nap time until, after a few days, she'd been told, he'd learned to be quiet then. She heard him singing with the others—he had a sweet, clear voice and appeared to love to sing, and he'd caught on fast to the songs "Michael Finnegan," "Waltzing Matilda," and "Crawdad Hole." Something calm and fun loving and beautiful about Farai seemed to speak to all who knew him.

He had to be safe somewhere. She couldn't lose her entire family.

61

It was two fifty when Chipo, Sue, and the deputy arrived at Sekai's apartment building and found Hannah's car and a sheriff's vehicle parked in front. A man sat at the wheel of an unmarked car parked just ahead of the others, a man vaguely familiar to Chipo from her son's class—one of the parents she thought. Bronson, Sims, Hannah, and this man appeared to be waiting for them. Detective Sims joined the three women and began to explain the situation. William Brost stood nearby, idling his motorcycle.

"Anything I can do to help Farai, I'm here," he told Chipo through the open car window.

"You tell me my son is inside with his teacher?" Chipo tried to open the locked door on her side of the car as she spoke to Sims.

"It might not be safe to go straight into the apartment where he's being held, Ms. Moyo," Sims told her. "We're thinking of your son's safety. I would prefer we telephone Ms. Nefas from the apartment next door. By the way, that's Mr. Chin from your son's day care center in the car ahead. Would you like us to telephone Ms. Nefas now?"

Chipo considered this silently, as was her wont, and he waited for her decision patiently. It was perhaps his plain clothes, but more likely his calm elder demeanor and being of her race that, after a moment, led her to give him a definite nod. Andrew Chin left his car and joined them as the deputy pushed the button to unlock the car doors and Chipo stepped out. The five—Chipo, Andrew, Sims, Sue, and Hannah—left William and the deputy with the cars and made their way through the propped-open outer door. They piled into the elevator and emerged at a run, speeding along the balcony to the apartment next door to Sekai's, where Sheriff Bronson awaited them.

The neighbor inside wore a paint-smeared apron, the room behind him filled with bold, up-close renditions of flowers and children. With his pointed goatee, skimpy shoulder-length gray hair, and a palette in one hand, he looked the epitome of an aged Parisian artist. He gave a gracious wave with his palette. "Anything for Sekai Turino," he told them. "She's a fine neighbor." Andrew grabbed the man's cordless phone and proceeded to call Joan next door.

"Joan, it's Andrew." His voice was gentle. "I'm very close to you now. If you come outside with Farai, I will meet you. I am prepared to discuss with you the matter you raised."

There was an outdoor passageway between the two apartments, and the sheriff and Sims crouched there. They had removed their guns from their holsters and held them with both hands, arms outstretched. The group inside stared intently at Andrew and awaited Joan's response.

There was a sudden loud crash as Joan, holding Sekai's cordless phone, flung open Sekai's door—the knob smashed into the wall and gouged the plaster. The sheriffs maintained their crouch, guns cocked. They all expected to encounter a violent woman holding Farai in front of her as a shield and making a desperate attempt to get away. But instead, Joan's mood seemed to swing as suddenly as she had appeared. The group peering out the artist's front door heard her subdued tone even as they saw her speak into Sekai's phone. "I'm coming out, Andrew," she told him, "and I'll bring Farai with me. His grandmother will accompany us."

Andrew glanced out the doorway at the sheriff and Sims. The three nodded at each other. Their tight, anxious bodies seemed to share one long, mutual exhalation.

"We're going next door for your son, Ms. Moyo," the sheriff told Chipo. "Do you feel strong enough to come with us?"

For answer, Chipo gave a scornful look as she strode out the artist's door. She sped the few feet down the balcony toward Joan and the two figures standing immediately behind her.

Later Chipo would say that she never in her life had felt such a combination of astonishment and joy as she had at the sight of her mother and son. Even the reality of Tapiwa's tragic death slipped away from her for this moment. She would mourn later, but now her strength was full and complete, and she wrapped her long, slender arms tightly around both figures, smiling, laughing, kissing. The others stood around the family in a protective circle, and they were the ones with tears in their eyes.

Chipo breathed the words softly: *"Mwari,* I thank you."

62

It was close to four o'clock when the excitement, surprise, and joy at Sekai's apartment began to abate. Andrew had returned to his bank, the sheriffs and Sims had taken Joan away, and Hannah had left for the center. When Sue left to return to her bungalow, Chipo stretched out on Sekai's sofa—Sekai worked late today with her babies at the center—while Farai straddled her ankles and listened to his mother and grandmother exchange breathless updates on all that had taken place. Then Farai stood close to Ruvimbo as she described Tapiwa's death the night before to her daughter. Chipo confided her anxiety about his political activities and the tragic fact that he had been about to move back with her and Farai that very evening.

The family didn't stop touching: Ruvimbo stroked Chipo's forehead; at one point Chipo buried her face in her mother's lap, while Ruvimbo combed her fingers through her daughter's abundant hair, one arm tightly around Farai. She explained to Chipo how Sekai had invited her here, and how her friend Tatenda had been able to gather the money for such a trip and procure a two-week visa. Chipo reached out to Farai, who climbed onto her lap. Tears rolled down his cheeks as he remembered the sudden terror and loss of the night before.

63

Hannah had left these three alone to begin the long healing process ahead. She felt giddy with relief over Farai's safety, exhilarated by his escape from danger, and throbbing with unwonted energy and excitement, though beneath these emotions she also felt deep fatigue. Playing over in her mind the day's events so far, she saw herself yoyo-like, shuttling between talks with one person, then another, culminating in the precarious confrontation with Joan and its miraculous resolution.

The question now burned in her mind: was Tapiwa's death an accident, or had someone, some*ones*, planned it to look that way? Bronson had seemed to feel it was a simple accident. Sims, on the other hand, had told her, "We can't be sure, Ms. Cooper. I'll be interviewing the bicyclist who hit Mr. Moyo, and the witnesses as well."

Was it an accident? The newspaper account presented it as such. But she couldn't forget the vivid description Chipo had given her the afternoon before, of the three countrymen who had threatened her in their search for Tapiwa. Could they have had something to do with his death? Perhaps they hired the bicyclist to knock him to the sidewalk. One read of deaths by hired killers. But using a bicycle? It seemed too uncertain a way to kill someone to be likely. And yet ...

Her thoughts seemed to etch deep, painful, circular grooves in her brain.

Drop on by if you have a free minute, Hannah. She heard Elaine's plaintive invitation of the morning sound in her memory as she neared the center again. She parked her car and without entering the center began to walk the quarter-mile across campus to Elaine's housing complex. As she walked she munched the battered power bar she kept in her purse. The chocolate and peanuts tasted stale, but she felt some renewal and her steps quickened. When had she last eaten? Ah yes, the apple just before Detective Sims had come this morning, an eternity ago.

Elaine's complex, one of the newer buildings on campus, looked solidly built and well maintained. Situated across the street from a small city park, it housed single graduate students. Hannah knew the institute had future plans for housing married students with children closer to campus, but no one seemed to know when and where that would happen.

To her surprise, an attractive young woman sat on the front steps of the building, almost as if she expected someone. Hannah stepped toward her.

"I'm Hannah Cooper, and I'm looking for—"

"Ms. Cooper! I'm so glad you're here." Elaine jumped to her feet, her right hand outstretched. "I didn't want to go up there alone," she told Hannah, and gestured to her apartment windows directly above the entrance. "I just feel so jumpy today."

The afternoon turned chilly as the sun neared the horizon beyond a clump of eucalyptus trees; their silver gray leaves shivered and rustled. Elaine unlocked the outer door to the building and led the way inside and to the elevator, and the two women proceeded to her door. Elaine laid her ear to it before she inserted her key; they heard her phone ring, but nothing more. She opened the door as the ringing ceased.

"I turned off my answer machine this morning," Elaine told Hannah. "I don't want any more scary Shona messages."

Hannah took in the surroundings where Farai's father had stayed the last few weeks of his life. Unconsciously, she'd imagined some kind of romantic love nest: soft, bright cushions, flowers, the smell of incense, maybe an Oriental rug, and harp and flute blending softly in the background, mellowing the whole.

What she saw instead appeared to be a highly organized work station. No clutter, no color except black and white. A slight fragrance of lemon detergent, perhaps. The chairs were bare wood, and no sofa softened the room. In the next room she could see a low double bed, neatly made up, the sheets tucked fiercely under the thin mattress. On the walls in both rooms were printouts of charts and equations—works in progress, as Hannah could see from the multicolored symbols and numbers that had been added by hand and the felt-tip markers spilled out onto a low table nearby.

She'd heard through the grapevine that this smart young woman knew what she wanted: success and fame in her field, along with a full professorship. Apparently, she kept the different sides of her life strictly compartmentalized. It probably disconcerted her when events exploded in her face. Hannah sat on one of the two stiff chairs and gave Elaine a friendly, expectant look.

"I've gone through a lot of changes this last year, Ms. Cooper," Elaine began, but Hannah interrupted with, "Please, call me Hannah."

"Okay, thank you, Hannah. I've been here at PTI for almost two years. Being one of the minority of women on campus is a story in itself, but I'll leave that alone for now.

"Mostly, I'm here because I love my work. But you know

how it can be—a woman does get lonely sometimes, and I had a guy live here with me last spring for a while."

What does this have to do with anything? Hannah made herself continue to listen.

"He was a loser, and I realized it pretty quick. But to deal with real people, not my numbers and work, can be tricky, and I didn't want to be mean to him, you know? He could fix anything that broke—my bike, the toaster, anything. But he had all kinds of trouble keeping up in lab, and it made him a bear to be around. At first I tried to help him, but that seemed to annoy him too."

Elaine gasped, interrupting herself. "Would you like tea or anything?" She sprang to her feet. When Hannah declined, she sat quickly again.

"So in May, I put him out. It turned out to be the very day his advisor told him they'd terminated his scholarship. He left here in a rage, I'll tell you.

"I had a lab assistantship to tide me over for the summer, and I only saw him once or twice after that, around town. He got a job at a computer repair shop. Actually, it was just right for him, but he hated it. It was a far cry from his glory dreams of success in theoretical science, all right." Elaine gave a brief laugh.

"I know you probably wonder why I'm spilling this out to you. Well, he's really on my mind today because he's the one who crashed into Tapiwa last night and killed him. I know he knew that Tapiwa lived with me this winter. He didn't know, though, that Tapiwa broke up with me yesterday morning, not that that matters here." She paused, and her next words came in a rush.

"Hannah, they say his crashing into Tapiwa and killing him is an accident, but I'm not so sure! George can be vindictive! He really knows how to hold a grudge." She gave Hannah an agonized glance.

"I didn't mention this to the sheriff this morning. Maybe I

should have—it just scares and humiliates me to bring up my love life with an armed man who's a stranger to me." Elaine clasped her hands as she looked directly at Hannah for a moment, and Hannah met her eyes with a brief nod.

"You're the only person I've told, though I guess maybe one or two of my friends here might put two and two together. I never went out socially on campus with either guy, but a few people might have known that first George, and then Tapiwa had lived with me.

"Not that anyone pays much attention to things like that around here. We're all mostly just into our work, and that stuff's not important." Her monologue now over, Elaine appeared relieved.

Not important. marveled Hannah over the age and culture gap between her and this young woman. She felt she'd come from another country, another time entirely. "How can I help?" she finally asked.

They talked some more and decided to call Detective Sims. Hannah punched in his number and left a message on his machine, telling him that she and Elaine Sark wanted to meet with him at his earliest convenience.

"Those three men from Tapiwa's country have me scared too, Hannah," Elaine told her. "They beat him up at home before he came here, he told me. He felt pretty sure his e-mail was under some kind of surveillance, and someone called him in the night here a couple of weeks ago. He wouldn't talk to me about it, but I could tell it scared him. "

"Campus security, as well as the sheriff's office, know about three African men harassing Tapiwa," Hannah told her. "I doubt they're a danger to you, but please, Elaine, stay inside and make sure your door's locked tonight."

"And you, Hannah? Do you feel safe walking back now to PCDC?"

64

Hannah left Elaine's in the late-afternoon January dark. She closed the self-locking door behind her and immediately heard rustling in the shrubs to her right. The last thing she noticed before a hand jammed her lips against her teeth was the smashed light bulb nearby. By the light of the emergency phone—the administration had installed these two months earlier in its safety beef-up—she saw that its cord was cut; the receiver lay on the grass nearby. These impressions scarcely registered as she felt her assailant's other hand reach for her throat. A gruff, sibilant voice shot into her right ear, "Be quiet if you know what's good for you."

It was her first-ever encounter with personal violence. She'd taken a self-defense class, but this was for real. She remembered, though: *stomp down backward and hard on the assailant's feet. Whirl around, two fingers in a V, and thrust them into the assailant's eyes. This will give you a moment's release. Use it to scream, and run like hell!*

The backwards stomp and the eye-punch worked. She ran panting toward the campus coffee shop nearby, seeing no one on the path. She could see people in the shop, though, and increased her speed.

Thud, thud. Footsteps. He had gained on her, and as she tasted salt and felt the wild thumping of her heart, she knew she was exhausted. A breather—she must have a breather.

She turned a corner and dived into some shrubbery. The administration had done a pretty good job of eliminating hiding places, but the oleanders here grew tall and thick. Her pursuer followed her around the corner, realized she'd hidden rather than sprinting the last distance to the coffee shop, and halted his steps. He stood still, panting hard, then crouched, looking and sniffing around him like a panther searching for its prey. She wished she hadn't dabbed oil of lavender behind her ears that morning. He would have smelled it during their encounter minutes before.

He surged in her direction, jerked to a stop, turned the opposite way where a dark building loomed, then leaped back toward her, forearms protecting his face from the snapping branches.

But she was running again now, on her second wind. Her inner voice offered odd comfort under the circumstances and brought a half smile to her lips as she sprinted: *I feel exhilarated!* the voice observed, as if ignoring what was really happening. Suddenly she heard his voice.

"Ms. Cooper, stop, please stop! It's me, George Vincent. I know you from the Computer Shack. I'm really sorry, Ms. Cooper! I thought you were somebody else. Only one woman lives in that building you came out of—"

She plunged into the coffee shop, threw herself into one of the chairs facing the door, and laid her head and arms on the table in front of her. Her entire body shook. She could feel the curious gazes of the few other patrons on the other side of the room. Then she heard the door open again—and saw him.

It was the young man who'd fixed her printer not long ago.

Anger burned through her, and for once in her life, she welcomed it. "You 'thought I was someone else'? And that makes it okay, is that what you meant?" she asked, her voice deadly cold. "You planned to kill Elaine, didn't you?"

"Aw, just scare her a little," he drawled, and her pulse raced higher. "Elaine's all right, but she can be such a bitch—pardon my language, Ms. Cooper." He sat down across the table from her and stretched his legs before him, seemingly unperturbed.

Hannah's tone, mustered from somewhere deep in her belly, matched his apparent casualness. "Mr. Vincent, why don't you tell me about how you came to kill Mr. Moyo last night?" At any other time she would not have believed she could speak so calmly.

"I don't have to tell you *nothing.*" George turned and looked behind him, gauging the distance between him and the doorway he'd entered, around seven or eight feet. Hannah wondered why he didn't run from this public place, indeed why he'd come in at all, but he stayed seated. In spite of his rudeness and his deadly physical threats a few moments earlier, he seemed to have a need to justify himself to her.

"It's like this, Ms. Cooper, about last night. I was riding my bike along Del Vista, minding my own business, and up ahead who do I see but this creep Teepee. That's not his real name, but he has a weird name something like that. He—" George fidgeted with his hands on the table between them. "He just looked like he was begging for trouble, so easy and comfortable with his little brat, like he was as good as anybody, know what I mean?"

She needed to hear this story, so she stayed still and willed herself to allow him to pour out this ugliness and hate, but she did not let it reach her core. To appear attentive and nonjudgmental at this moment was one of the hardest things she'd ever done. At least she felt physically safe—the other patrons had resumed their laughter and conversation.

"So what happened next, Mr. Vincent?" she breathed.

He seemed hardly aware of her, talking instead to—whom? Himself? A feared schoolteacher from his grade school days? His mother or father perhaps?

"I just thought I could maybe teach him a little respect. I was going real fast, see? And it was dark, except for the light from the pizza stand generator. So I got up speed, you know, and then I just jammed my brakes on the gravel—I had to brace myself to keep from going over the handlebars—and *smashed* into that little ole generator."

Hannah could see the entire scene George was describing, and her stomach turned over as she gripped the sides of her chair.

"Pop! The lights went out just like that! It was great! And then I just let myself skid, you know, skid right into that creep! *Unh!* Crunch! But I din't mean no harm to him, not really, you know. Just wanted to rough him up a little bit, you know?"

His face crumpled suddenly, and for a split second Hannah thought he might feel remorse. Then, with a crafty expression, he lowered his voice and told her, "You'd better stay in here all night, lady, 'cause you and Elaine are the only ones know I might've had a reason to kill that bastard. I'm a patient man. I'll wait for you.

"Oh, and by the way." He fumbled a bloodstained rabbit's paw from his pants pocket, reached across the table, and waved it in Hannah's face. "Thanks for this little souvenir, Ms. Cooper!" He jumped up and, walking like a cat on the balls of his feet, headed for the door behind him, throwing it open to the night outside as Hannah gazed after him.

Suddenly there was blinding light and he was thrown into silhouette. She heard a voice boom: "Don't move, Vincent. We've got you covered. Let us see your hands."

65

"Hannah, this is Harold, Assemblyman Harold Moore, do you remember me?"

So present, so friendly. Hannah suspended her amazement. "Yes, certainly. Maureen Brady and I visited you a couple of weeks ago—about AB four sixty-nine. How is your son?"

"You remembered that, Hannah—thanks! Matthew's okay. We had a terrible scare, but he knew the kids who had threatened him. We were able to talk with the principal at his school and get the three boys into his office. Not easy for Matthew, I'll tell you, but the principal insisted the boys talk through what happened. We found out they only live a few blocks from us. The principal called in the parents after the boys talked—two mothers, no dads on the scene, plus me and my wife. The moms were scared and angry at first, and my wife and I were angry too, you can imagine.

"But we figured out a deal, and I think it just might be working." A fit of coughing stopped him momentarily, and Hannah could hear children's voices behind him.

"My wife and I decided we'll stay on Madison Avenue where we are and work with this thing. She's started to volunteer in the classrooms at the school, like my mom did there, not so many years back."

"I'm so pleased to hear this, Harold! Here at the center we work hard to help kids communicate. It gets harder when they're older, but the principal at your middle school sounds good at what he does. You and your wife are certainly to be congratulated for hanging in, in a very tough situation."

"Right. Well actually, that's not what I called you about, Hannah. I got that notice you sent out about how someone killed your pet rabbit and you're holding a meeting tonight for the center parents with someone from the sheriff's department there, and I—well, I'd like to come too, Hannah, and say a few words about building our neighborhoods, getting involved. Would that be possible?"

Again she swallowed her amazement. Something that felt like bubbles of delight floated up from her gut toward her throat, causing serious eye moisture. "I'm pretty sure I can get campus clearance for that, Harold. We start at seven this evening. Three others are already on the panel, and the parents' time is limited because they need to get their kids to bed. Can you keep your remarks brief?"

Moore agreed, and Hannah alerted Kevin Drabb, who approved his presence at the meeting. She lost no time in calling Maureen and some of the other EC advocates around town. It was only a start, but it felt glorious.

66

April 1999

"Chipo," Sue asked, "have you heard anything lately from Alexis about your status?" *She's thinner than before*, Sue realized with a pang.

They sat on a bench on the PTI campus and shared their brown bag lunches. Sue had arranged the get-together a few days earlier, and she expected Hannah soon. A rounded green sculpture partly encircled them, one of several such pieces scattered along carefully landscaped knolls and sweeping lawns. On this mild day the undulating stone gave them a sense of protection and privacy. Behind them a fountain plashed, steady and gentle. The sun warmed them just enough to make it enjoyable to sit outdoors.

"Yes, it looks as if my mother, Farai, and I will head home soon," Chipo told her. "The institute is arranging our air passage. How I wish we could stay! But the law is very strict. Everyone has been kind, and no one from the United States government has come after me or detained me during these last three months. But since I'm here alone now, I have no legal status. Alexis has been wonderful about getting the fellowship payments continued for Farai and me while we've gotten ourselves together, and she's helping us extend my mother's visa as well."

"I know you've cleaned houses for some of the PCDC parents. It makes my heart ache to see you doing such work!" Sue burst out.

"I felt that way, too, at first, but the cash is good. And mindless work like that, you know, dusting and vacuuming and washing dishes, it frees the mind. I've been able to think a lot, and—how do you say?—grieve."

"Will you and Farai be safe in Zimbabwe?" Sue's voice trembled.

"Maybe no. But perhaps it is true that one is not completely safe anywhere, Sue? Once I am home, I may walk across the western border, to Botswana. They say it is safer there. In Botswana, they speak Setswana, and I understand it pretty well. Many Zimbabwean people are doing this now, walking across the borders. I think I can get a job in a large clinic I've heard about there."

"You mean an AIDS clinic? I've heard how so many people both in Zimbabwe and in Botswana are AIDS victims."

"Yes, an AIDS clinic, but one well enough funded to be able to practice safe hygiene. Working there should not increase my risk of AIDS."

"And what about your mother?"

"I hope she'll join us. She has a friend in Harare, a peddler who lent her the money to come here. Perhaps he'll come with her. We'll have to take things one at a time."

Chipo paused, reflected, then continued: "At first I wanted to stay here in the United States, but my thoughts have changed on this. Tapiwa would have wanted us to return to Zimbabwe to try to help build a safer community there, but I cannot endanger Farai in that way. So perhaps Botswana will be a third way, safer than Zimbabwe, closer than America."

Hannah joined the two women and gave them each a quick hug. She immediately asked Chipo, "How have these months been for you?"

"Farai and I are healing, Hannah. I've had time to think, time to get to know my mother again," Chipo began, "and Sekai has been a big help, too, a second grandma for Farai.

"But you, Hannah, I've wanted to ask you this. How did you know of George Vincent's connection with my Tapiwa?"

"Really, it was Elaine who made the connection. She and I talked that day. Then when she looked out her window and saw George attack me she called the sheriff's office. Later, she took her courage in her hands and told them about George's connection, through her, with Tapiwa—probably the hardest thing she's ever done."

"And will he be brought to justice?" Another of Sue's direct questions.

"I'm told that life imprisonment's likely. George didn't premeditate what he did, so he'll probably be sentenced for second-degree murder. He could get fifteen years to life for that. But his attack on me *was* premeditated—even though he thought he was stalking Elaine that night."

For a few moments the three women digested these outward results of the wrenching experiences they'd survived.

Sue realized how fond she'd become of Chipo, her quiet reserve, her deep, warm laugh, her strength, her clipped British speech. "Have you thought about staying in the United States underground, Chipo? Alan and I would try to help you if you did, and you have many other friends here too, you know."

"You're a dear friend, Sue, and how kind you are!" Chipo shed no tears; she had shed many these last months, but lately a new clarity steadied her with Farai, and even opened her eyes to the beauty of spring in Pasadena, the blossoming fruit trees, the jacarandas that reminded her of home, the magnolias her bus passed on its way to PCDC each morning with her son.

"I learned from my mother as a little girl that life can be

good even after a terrible loss, and we can move forward." Her words were firm and she touched her hand to her breast as she said them one by one.

"It is my turn to ask you, Sue, how are you?" Chipo looked at her friend expectantly. "I know you are happy about the baby coming. Are you happy other ways too?"

"How can I put it into words?" Sue asked both women. "I hardly know myself! It's good to have Alan home again, good to have gotten pregnant so soon after his return. My dissertation's on the back burner now—I packed the books and papers into a box. It meant so much to me at one time—now this new life seems to have blotted it out. I never would have thought that could happen." She appeared to want their responses.

"Emily will wait a while, Sue—dead poets are patient!— and you may find later on that the research and writing go much more quickly. It's funny how things work out like that sometimes!" Not for the first time, Hannah contemplated the vulnerability of young mothers and fathers in their twenties and thirties, learning about life in ways almost as basic as the ways a young child learns. How well she remembered her own roller-coaster years of early parenting!—and what a challenge she found it to try to pass on some of the wisdom she'd gained with such difficulty.

A woman walked quickly across their line of vision. Her expression was stony and she looked straight ahead. They watched her disappear into one of the buildings to their left. Chipo broke the silence of the three on the bench.

"That was Joan, wasn't it? Farai still speaks of her! Are you at liberty to tell us what happened to her after that dreadful day?"

Hannah looked toward where Joan had disappeared into the science building. "You already know all too well how deeply troubled Joan was when she held your son and mother hostage. After such an act, a teacher could never be permitted to work again with children. And the sheriff did hold her for seventy-two hours. They can do that when someone appears mentally unbalanced but isn't a danger to others."

"Isn't a danger to others! But what about Farai, before his rescue? And what about Ruvimbo?" Sue broke in.

"Joan had no weapon, and she was very subdued when Andrew, Detective Sims, the sheriffs, and Chipo arrived at Sekai's apartment. You remember, Sue? You were there too."

"They asked me if I wanted to press charges," Chipo spoke. "And I told them I just wanted my son. Of course I also never wanted to see Joan again, but I didn't tell them that."

Hannah spoke up. "Andrew and some others in the community who valued her past services put together some help for Joan, and she's been faithful about the therapy and job training sessions they arranged for her. I don't know if you know that before she began to teach, she used to manage sales in a large firm back east. She has experience and skills, and I understand that PTI has found her an administrative job in one of the larger labs, where she's doing quite well." Hannah was trying to be objective, though her insides hurt.

"She's on probation, of course, like any new hire, but if she can stay steady, she may wind up not only better paid, but happier than before."

"I know it's none of my business," Sue asked, "but have you and she ever talked since that day?"

"You do ask the most direct questions, Sue! It's okay, though—we've been through a lot together, haven't we? But to answer you, no, I think Joan will never forgive me for what she sees as the unfair treatment she received at PCDC. I'm glad the sheriff stopped her that day before she did any lasting harm, and glad that Andrew could get some help for her."

"Not lasting harm, Hannah, holding Farai and his grandmother hostage?" Sue's mouth tightened. "I can't believe you're saying that!"

"I know what you think, Sue, but here's why he wasn't truly harmed. Ruvimbo shielded him that day in the most phenomenal way." Chipo paused. Her eyes softened as she chuckled. "You know how my mother described Joan, later on? *Anopenga!* meaning 'she was crazy.'

"My mother is fierce! She was not about to let anyone touch him. It was she, you know, who seized him the night before, when Tapiwa was killed. She took him, in Sekai's car, to Sekai's home. She and Sekai were at the pizza stand, in Sekai's car, their eyes on Farai and Tapiwa, when it happened."

"Are you saying his bond of trust with her protected him?"

Chipo nodded confirmation to Sue. "Yes, Farai really hasn't seriously suffered from the Joan episode. My mother remained close by him the whole time that Joan held them, and she stayed sturdy, so Farai did too. To think I had to come to the United States to learn who my mother is and how much I appreciate her! Even though I miss Tapiwa so much, I have to chuckle at myself." And Chipo laughed again, a long, happy sound.

Music to our ears, thought Hannah, *to hear Chipo laugh. Healing has begun. It's happening.*

"His father's death, though, that has been his real sorrow." Chipo cleared her throat and continued. "And as for me, I admire Tapiwa and love him more than I did when he lived. Is it not strange?"

Another silence fell, broken by Sue. "We'll miss you terribly, Chipo, but we'll help you get ready for your trip, and we'll stay in touch when you're home again, and maybe—who knows?— Alan can get a research grant for somewhere in southeast Africa, somewhere near your country, and maybe we can get the boys together again!"

Chipo leaned back and stretched her arms above her head, then half turned and hugged her friend, her voice somber. "Miracles sometimes happen."

67

Los Angeles
Thursday, January 21, 1999

Crenshaw Boulevard south of Slauson, six fifteen Thursday morning. Cracks in the ancient stucco ooze brown mud. Crushed remnants of beer and soda cans are visible beneath bark chips covering the weedy, eroded berm in front of the row of motel units. Inside Number Five, two young black men are stiff even in sleep, their toes lined up with their chins. Stained take-out boxes litter the floor, and the room stinks of stale tobacco, though these young men do not smoke. The even breath of one complements that of the other. If a breath quickens for one, the other's speeds up, and if one coughs, the other's breath pauses. They form a unit, bonded in this strange land. They will watch out for each other.

As for the older man who is part of their group, he, after all, is not of the *now*; he is part of *then* and must be understood as such. One cannot simply accept and act on his pronouncements; one must evaluate them. It is a dilemma for the younger men because their leader at home has given clear instructions about this mission of watching over Tapiwa, of ensuring Tapiwa's return in twenty months to Zimbabwe. They have been instructed to give absolute loyalty to the older man. It is a dilemma, yes, but for now they sleep, though their eyes are only half shut.

Quick footsteps outside, a key turns in the lock, and the door opens soundlessly. Newspaper rustles as the older man enters, closes the door, and hurls the *Los Angeles Times,* folded open to an inner page, onto the stained satin bedspread.

"Men!" He shakes them hard, and they both spring to sitting position, eyes wide open and staring ahead. Their right hands bang their foreheads in stiff salutes.

"Sir?"

"You were the cause of this! We have lost our man! We were to harass and threaten Tapiwa—we were not to kill him! Always your young blood wants to hurt and kill. I know you, you were jealous of him, you took your revenge through this white man, this bicyclist—"

He grabs the paper, crumples it, throws it back on the bed.

One of the young men seizes it, smoothes it open, and finds the tiny news note about Tapiwa's death the night before. He reads it to his friend. The two exchange a long look and without words agree on what they will say.

"Sir, we did have Tapiwa killed, but not for revenge, not for jealousy. We did it because of his traitorous desire to stay in this country, to not come back. We learned of this yesterday at the Internet café, while you got the fried chicken for us. Tapiwa had e-mailed one of his fellow dissidents at home—he used that code that he thinks safe but that we understand. He told his friend his wife did not want to return. We ..."

"You did not consult me! You did not even tell me!" The older man's breath comes loud and hard, and his voice rasps.

"Sir, we have the e-mail." One of them produces the faded printout and hands it to the older man, who pulls out his glasses, wipes them, and places them on his large nose with fingers that, they notice, tremble.

The coded message is unmistakable. Chipo does not wish to return to Zimbabwe in the year 2000. Tapiwa confides this to his friend in Harare. The e-mail also refers to a secret coup attempt on Mugabe in December.

"We thought, sir, if we dispatched him now, it would be best, and that if we acted without your knowledge, this would be best for you at home, sir."

The older man considers. Yes, possibly something in what the youngsters say is worth his attention. It was a traitor they killed, after all, and he would be commended for this when they returned. Their youth would pardon their acting alone, and their acting alone ensured that he would not be blamed for the distortion of their mission. He does not like what they have done, but perhaps it is for the best.

He says nothing, only gives a brief nod and proceeds to the bathroom, where he washes his hands repeatedly.

The two young men nod and smile behind his back. He believes them! They will be heroes.

LaVergne, TN USA
10 November 2009
163623LV00001B/2/P